Being in Quinn, Texas, at night was as different from being in Chicago as being on another planet,

Jasmine thought as she sat on the porch swing.

The creak of the screen door and heavy footfalls spoke of Luke's approach even before he sat down beside her. He gave a push of his big boots and sent the swing into motion. Then he crossed his arms behind his head and leaned back, stretching out his long legs.

"You know, you've got to stop running sometime. Some*where*. Sooner or later, you have to fight this thing. And here is where you have the best shot at beating it. Here, Jasmine. You can win here."

Lifting her gaze slowly, she searched his eyes. "What makes here so much different than anywhere else?"

He pinned her with a piercing stare. "I'm here."

* * *

"Shayne gives readers a rich, sensual and bewitching adventure of good vs. evil, with love as the prize."

—*Publishers Weekly*

Coming soon from national bestselling author

MAGGIE SHAYNE

More stories featuring the fabulous Brand family!

Look for the new series

The excitement began with

**THE BRANDS WHO CAME
FOR CHRISTMAS**
(IM #1039, November 2000)

Look for BRAND-NEW HEARTACHE (IM #1117)
coming in December 2001

Also available in December 2001
from Silhouette Books:

WINGS IN THE NIGHT

Three spellbinding novels
in one exhilarating volume!

MAGGIE SHAYNE

★★★★★★★★★★★ THE TEXAS BRAND ★★★★★★★★★★★

THE HOMECOMING

Silhouette Books

Published by Silhouette Books
America's Publisher of Contemporary Romance

SILHOUETTE BOOKS

RECYCLED PAPER · RECYCLED PAPER

THE TEXAS BRAND: THE HOMECOMING

Copyright © 2001 by Margaret Benson

ISBN 0-373-48429-1

This edition published by arrangement with Harlequin Books S.A.

Visit Silhouette at www.eHarlequin.com

Printed in U.S.A.

To Eileen Fallon, my agent, mentor and, most important, dear friend.

Chapter 1

Luke stood at the graveside of his best friend and mentor, the man he'd always wanted to emulate, and waited for the others to arrive—but they never did. The minister stood there, too. He was a small, skinny man with a road map of a face. He didn't wear flowing robes, though. The only things that marked him as a man of the cloth were the collar of his shirt and the Bible in his hand. It was a pretty day in Tennessee. Birds singing. Traffic rushing by. Flowers in bloom. Just like nothing had ever happened. Just like the greatest long-distance trucker in the business wasn't lying dead right now in a box about to be lowered into the cold womb of the earth.

The minister looked at his watch, then at Luke.

"Are you sure we're not early?" Luke asked. He'd expected hundreds to be in attendance. Buck was a legend. A favorite of every truck-stop waitress and diesel mechanic in seven states. His rig had been the most recognizable one on the road, all decked out with chrome, and more lights than a Christmas tree. Oh, it had been a showpiece. Buck's pride and joy.

It twisted Luke's stomach to think of the way it had looked when he'd stopped by the wrecking yard to view the remains. Just a pile of twisted metal and shattered glass. Nothing left of its former glory.

And now it looked to Luke as though there was even less left of its owner-operator. It bothered him that no one had come to say goodbye to Buck.

The minister cleared his throat and met Luke's eyes. Luke sighed and gave him a nod. The preacher began to speak, but he didn't really have much to say. He read the Lord's Prayer, said how Buck had gone on to a better place. He talked about salvation. Luke listened until he couldn't listen anymore. Then he said, "'Scuse me, Reverend, but um...do you think it would be all right if I, uh..."

The man smiled, new wrinkles appearing in his face. "By all means, son. Say a few words. Lord knows, you knew this man better than I."

Nodding, Luke cleared his throat. He held his hat, a duck-billed green one that had a bulldog and the word *Mack* on the front, in his hands in front of him. "Lord," he said, "this man was one of the good ones. I suppose you know that already, but I want to make sure it gets said. He never passed by a broken-down four-wheeler on the roadside without stopping to offer a hand. He never left a hitchhiker out in the rain. He never left less than a dollar tip for a waitress, even if all he ordered was a cup of coffee. And there was never a better driver. Not ever. Why, I've seen Buck Waters perform acrobatics with his rig when he lost his brakes on a three-mile downgrade, when any other driver would have wound up jackknifing and taking a lot of people with him. I've seen him pull out of a slide on roads so icy you couldn't walk on them. I've seen him avoid accidents that would have killed anyone else, when ignorant folks pulled out in front of him or cut him off. In fact, he never did have a wreck—not until this one. Now, I know it doesn't seem like much of a legacy to leave behind. But it's all he had. And I sure hope you won't hold that against him. Some men just aren't cut out for settling down, raising families and all that. And just because no one's here today, no kids or wife crying at the graveside...well, that doesn't mean Buck Waters wasn't loved. He was. And it doesn't mean he didn't touch lives. Because he touched mine."

Luke lowered his head as a flood of feeling rushed up into his throat and kept him from saying more.

A soft hand fell on his shoulder. "That was very eloquent, son."

He glanced up at the minister, pulled himself together and shook his head. "It's not right that no one's here for him. There should have been lots of people here today."

The older man's brows rose. "Well, you're here." He paused a moment, deep in thought. "From what you've said about your friend, it seems his life was as full as he wanted it to be. Maybe so is this service."

"No," Luke said, shaking his head. "Every man wants to think someone's going to miss him when he's gone. Every man wants to leave something of himself behind."

Smiling very gently, the minister said, "No, son. Not every man. But it's pretty obvious *you* want those things."

"Me? No. No, not me."

The minister looked at the shiny coffin and smiled sadly. "Maybe this service is Buck's way of reminding you that you won't get those things in the end if you live the way he did. Family. Loved ones. Oh, I'm sure for him his life was perfect without those things. But maybe…yours isn't?" He shrugged. "It's something to think about, at any rate."

Luke frowned but said nothing. A million disjointed thoughts were spinning in his head. Above them all was the voice of his mother, telling him he would never settle down, that he had been born with the wanderlust, just like his father.

The minister turned again to the open grave and held one hand, palm out, above it. "Lord, we commend the soul of Buck Waters into thy tender care. May his soul fly on wings of angels into heaven. Amen."

"Amen," Luke intoned. "Hammer down, Buck."

The minister patted Luke again as he left. Luke spent a few more moments in the cemetery. Then he headed into the parking lot, where his rig took up most of the spaces. It gleamed like a gem, that rig of his. A turquoise-blue Pete, with a sleeper the size of a condo. Had a fridge, a microwave, TV and VCR. He could live in it. Hell, he did, a lot of the time. The polished Aluminum Bud wheels all the way around shone in the sunlight. On the side, in silver lettering, was his name. Lucas Tyrel Mason Brand, Owner-Operator. The rig was running, flaps on top of the twin smokestacks clicking up and down as if talking to him. You didn't just shut a semi down for a brief stop and start it up again like you would with a car. You let her idle. Let her purr. It was good for her.

Luke climbed behind the wheel, closed his hands around its familiar shape. And he told himself he wasn't all that much like Buck. Sure, his life was on the road, hauling loads of goods from town to town, state to state. He didn't really have a home.

But, unlike Buck, he had family. Well...relatives, anyway. His daddy's wandering ways had seen to that. The man had been married to two women at the same time. Fathered two kids on the East Coast and five in Oklahoma before he died in a hail of gunfire twenty-some odd years ago. Luke had no real memory of John Brand. His own mother hadn't been a wife at all, legal or otherwise. She'd just been a fling. And Luke had been the result of it. Still, John Brand's name was listed on Luke's birth certificate. And the old bastard had sent money, even come to visit several times a year until he'd been killed, according to Luke's mother. Not that Luke had much memory of the man himself, but his mother had always been very honest about it all. And when she passed last year she'd made Luke promise to visit his seven half siblings and all those cousins in Texas—the children of John Brand's brother, Orrin.

Of course he hadn't done it. Hadn't seen any reason to. Until now.

He drew a deep breath, sighed heavily. He supposed having relatives didn't really mean a hell of a lot if you'd never met them. Still, it was a daunting prospect. What was he supposed to do? Just pull the big rig into some stranger's driveway and yell, "Hi there, I'm your illegitimate bastard half brother."

His mobile phone rang. He picked it up. "Lucas Brand Trucking," he said automatically.

"Hey, Luke, it's me. How was the funeral?" The voice on the other end belonged to Smitty, one of Luke's favorite brokers.

"Not too good, Smitty. But I suppose funerals aren't supposed to be."

"Guess not. Look, I know this is a bad time, but I've got a load bound for Texas, Luke. And it needs to go out today. Can you take it?"

Luke swallowed hard. Texas. Of all places. Odd coincidence, just when he'd been thinking about the relatives he'd never met. "Where in Texas?" he asked.

"Town called Quinn. It's in the neighborhood of El Paso," Smitty said.

The words fell on Luke like bricks. He just sat there a minute, blinking in shock.

"Luke?"

"You've gotta be kidding me," Luke finally managed to say. "Quinn? You said Quinn, Texas?"

"No, I'm not kidding. Why, what's wrong with Quinn? Look, the call just came in, Luke. I guess your friend Buck was slated to take this load today, but, uh...well, with the accident and all..."

"Buck? This was Buck's run?"

"Yeah. Is that too, you know, morbid for you, Luke?"

Luke closed his eyes. In his mind he heard the minister's words of only a few moments before. *Maybe this is Buck's way of reminding you that you*

*won't get those things in the end if you live the way
he did....*

Buck had never steered Luke wrong in his life.
He'd been the father figure Luke had never had—
had never even known he *wanted*. And crazy as it
might seem, Luke had the feeling Buck was trying
to guide him just one last time. It didn't make any
sense to think that way. Hell, he wasn't even sure
he believed in life after death. But...but he couldn't
not do this. It was almost like Buck's last request.

"I'll take the load," he said finally.

"Great," Smitty said. "Luke, is there anywhere
in particular you want to head from there? I can
hook you up with an outgoing load if you want,"

Luke licked his lips. "Let's leave this one open-
ended. I might, um...I might be staying there a
while."

He heard the surprise in the other man's voice
when Smitty said, "Oh. Okay, sure, Luke, whatever
you want. The load you're hauling out there is fer-
tilizer. Pick it up at the Farm-Rite Depot on Eaton
and Main. Can you find that?"

"Yeah," Luke said. "I can find it." He hung up
the phone, glancing back toward the cemetery and
the grave of his friend. "Hell, Buck, I suppose
you're taking it easy on me. Cousins in Texas are
going to be a lot easier to start off with than a pile
of half sisters in Oklahoma."

Drawing a deep breath, he revved the engine, released the brake and slid the truck into gear.

Halfway there, Luke decided it might not be a bad idea to call these poor unsuspecting cousins in Quinn, Texas, and let them know he existed and would be in town for a visit soon. He had a momentary bout of panic when the operator told him there were five Brands listed in Quinn.

"Five?" He downshifted, cradling the phone between his ear and shoulder.

He didn't have a clue.

"Do you know the address?" the operator asked.

"No. Only that it's some kind of a ranch."

"There's a dude ranch...."

"No, it's a regular ranch. Cattle, I think." He racked his brain to recall the name. His mom had mentioned it once, he was sure she had.

"I have two ranches. Sky Dancer Ranch, and The Texas Brand," the operator said.

"That's it. The Texas Brand." He swallowed hard. "Can you connect me?"

Luke didn't know what to expect, really. The man on the phone, Garrett Brand, had been surprised but kind, and he'd seemed welcoming. He'd even given Luke directions to the ranch from the depot in town and asked him what time they could expect him. But Luke was still nervous. In his experience, in his entire life, the word *family* had almost no meaning. It was him and his mother. And sure, they'd been close, but in more of an "us against the world" kind of way. His mother had never let anyone else into their world. Friends, neighbors, they were held at arm's length. His mother had told him over and over again that they didn't need anyone else. That they would be fine all on their own. She'd been a strong, fiercely proud woman who couldn't seem to trust. And maybe that had a lot to do with his father, and maybe there was more to it. Luke didn't know and probably never would. But in his experience, family meant, "hands off." It was a tight, closed relationship that did not welcome outsiders.

So when he pulled his rig into the dusty curving driveway, underneath the huge wooden arch that had "Texas Brand" carved into its face, Luke was totally unprepared for what awaited him.

It had only been four hours since he'd made that phone call. Yet a huge banner was draped from the wide front porch of the white ranch house. "Welcome Luke" was hand-painted in crooked letters across its face. Between that and the place where he brought his rig to a stop there must have been twenty people milling around amid picnic tables loaded with food.

His throat tightened up a little as he shut the rig down, opened his door and climbed out. When he looked up, a big man stood in front of him, wearing a ten-gallon hat and a warm smile. He reached out and clasped Luke's hand. "I'm Garrett," he said. "Welcome to the family, Luke." His grip was firm and dry, and he shook Luke's hand with enthusiasm.

Luke shook his head. "I didn't expect all this," he said. "You shouldn't have gone to all this fuss."

"Hey, it isn't every day we get a new member of the family," a dark-skinned man said. He grinned and nodded toward the woman on his arm, whose belly was swollen. "Although in a few months, we'll be getting a couple more, right, Elliot?"

Across the way another man, this one with reddish-brown hair, hugged his own woman to his side, and she, too, looked to be expecting. "Right you are, Wes. Three months, two weeks and three days, if Doc's accurate."

Wes shook Luke's hand, introducing his wife, Taylor, and then Elliot followed suit, along with his wife, Esmeralda. The next man to come up to him was as big as Garrett, but blond, and his wife was a bit of a thing named Penny, who cradled a baby boy in her arms. Then there were the handsome Adam and his wife Kirsten, who looked to Luke like they should be modeling western wear in a magazine. And then there was a fellow named Lash and his wife Jessi.

Finally yet another woman parted the crowd to bring two kids front and center. A strapping boy of six or so, and a little girl who couldn't have been more than three, stood right in front of Luke. The woman said, "I'm Chelsea, Garrett's wife. This is my son, Bubba, and Jessi's little girl, Maria-Michelle. And they have something for you.''

His head spinning, Luke hunkered down to more of a level with the kids. The little girl was just as pretty as a picture, and she held up a box to him. The little boy unfolded a piece of paper, and everyone around went silent as he cleared his throat.

> "In our family, we have one rule
> Bigger than all the rest,
> Family comes first, and family is best!
> So welcome to our family,
> We're happy that you came.
> But you need just one more thing
> That goes with the family name.''

The little boy looked up shyly. "I wrote it myself. Mom helped.''

"I don't know when I've heard a nicer poem, Bubba. Thanks.''

The little girl shoved the box at him and said, "I helped whap it! I put on the bow!''

"And a beautiful bow it is,'' Luke said, taking the package. He opened it carefully, sticking the bow to his shirt pocket and seeing the little girl smile even wider. Then he took the lid off the box to find a soft brown Stetson hat inside.

He swallowed hard, taking it out of the box and turning it slowly, admiring its perfect shape and its hand-tooled leather band. "This is just...too much. You guys are..."

"Put it on!" Bubba said.

Luke looked at the men around him. Most of them wore hats like this one, the colors varied, of course. Slowly he took off his Mack hat and replaced it with the Stetson. Then he straightened.

A whoop went up, and then everyone was talking at once, slapping his back and tugging him toward the food. Someone turned on some country music. He smelled barbecue and smoke. And he felt...hell, he couldn't say just what he felt. It was as if his heart were swelling up in his chest. He hadn't known he could have this. He still couldn't believe it was for real. That these people wouldn't all just finish the show they were putting on for him and then send him on his way, and that would be the last he ever heard from them.

He was wrong about that, of course. Three months later he was still there, and for the first time in his life, he was part of a huge, open-armed, loving, real, honest-to-goodness family. And every night before he went to sleep, he whispered his thanks to his old friend Buck Waters for somehow leading Luke to what Buck himself had never had.

Chapter 2

Jasmine did not like having her son anywhere near the dive where she waited tables and occasionally danced on them. She didn't even like having Baxter in this part of Chicago. But once again, her low-life boss had forgotten to mail her paycheck, along with her roommate's, so she'd had no choice but to stop and pick them up. She pulled the car into the employee parking area in the back. There was not another vehicle in sight, and she considered that a good thing, given the kinds of people who tended to congregate at The Catwalk. Of course, most of them would be comatose at this time of the morning. Sighing, she turned to Baxter.

He sat in the passenger seat, looking up at her through the round lenses of his glasses. Seven years old, and already his teachers were suggesting he skip ahead a grade. He was fully smart enough to understand why he should do as she told him. He seldom did, however.

"Now listen to me," she said, and she made her voice as stern as it had ever been when speaking to her reason for being. "I have to get my paycheck so we can stop at the bank on the way to school and get you some cash for that end-of-the-year field trip today. All right?"

He nodded, pushing his glasses up on his nose with his forefinger. "And you have to get Aunt Rosebud's check, too."

"I know."

"And her bag, too, Mom. Don't forget her bag," he reminded her.

"I won't forget." She touseled her son's hair. "Your crazy Aunt Rosebud would forget her own head if it wasn't attached, wouldn't she?"

He giggled. "Nobody could forget their head," he said, though he was smiling. "But, yeah, she sure does forget things a lot."

Yes, she did. But last night, at least, she'd had reason for her customary absentmindedness. Jasmine's roommate had received a phone call last night from a lawyer, telling her that her mother had died shortly after she'd taken off. He'd been searching for Rosebud ever since. And even though Rosebud hadn't seen the woman in two years, the news had still hit her hard. Jasmine wanted to help, but she didn't know how. She and Rosebud were more like sisters than roommates. They worked together, lived together, shared their car, their expenses... even Baxter. Before Rosebud, Jasmine had never been willing to let any other human being into her world. It was just her and her son—no one else needed, wanted or welcome, thank you very much. But Rosebud had somehow worked her way into Jasmine's heart. It was good to have a friend. Someone you could trust. And it drove Jasmine crazy that she hadn't been able to ease the pain in Rosebud's eyes last night.

"Mom?"

Blinking, Jasmine brought her focus back to the matter at hand. Baxter. "Now, listen close, honey, it's only going to take me a minute to run into that building, grab the checks—"

"And Aunt Rosebud's bag."

"And Aunt Rosebud's bag, and run right back out again. I want you to *wait right here*. It's *very* important. Okay?"

Baxter nodded again. But already his attention was being pulled away from her, his big eyes straying as he scanned the parking area, the buildings, the pigeons on the roofs, the trash cans near Leo's office window, the rear entrance to the bar. "If there were an owl back here, there wouldn't be so many pigeons hanging around," Baxter said casually.

"That's good, Baxter. I'll be sure to tell my boss

that, but you need to pay attention to what I'm telling you now."

"No rats, either. Owls are their natural predators."

"Yes, that's true."

"We need more owls around here." He nodded thoughtfully, as if certain he'd just solved one of Chicago's biggest problems. Then he looked at her in all seriousness and said, "Can I drive the rest of the way to school?"

"You can't even reach the pedals!"

"Can so! Aunt Rosebud let me drive in the parkin' lot one day!" Then he clapped a hand over his mouth, and his eyes widened. Obviously he wasn't supposed to tell that little secret.

"Aunt Rosebud lets you do just about whatever you want," Jasmine said softly. "That doesn't mean I'm gonna let you do the same. Now, do you promise to stay in the car like I told you and be a good boy for a minute, so I can get those checks?"

"And Aunt Rosebud's bag," he gently reminded her. "Yes, I'll be good."

"Promise?"

He nodded solemnly. "Spit-swear!" he said, and he spat into his palm and offered it to her to shake.

"Where do you pick this stuff up, Bax? Look, a promise is a promise. I don't need a spit-swear, okay?"

He made a face. "Okay." Then he wiped his palm on his jeans.

Jasmine locked his door, then got out and locked her own before she closed it. She blew him a kiss and headed to the bar's back door, but when she tried to open it, it wouldn't give. Locked. Damn. She would have to go around to the front. A cold shiver danced up her spine the second her car and her son were out of her sight. "It'll only be a minute," she told herself. "He'll be fine." But she didn't like him being here. Not in this neighborhood, much less in this bar. She'd be damned before she would take him inside with her.

She walked through the front door, underneath the neon sign that read The Catwalk. On the walls were photos of mostly naked women in various poses. The round tables were clean, their chairs upside down on top of them. She waited tables here four nights a week. On weekends she danced. The stage was empty now except for the poles she and Rosebud and a couple of other girls twined themselves sensuously around on Friday and Saturday nights while music pounded and men howled. She never took *everything* off. And she never turned tricks, though several of the other dancers did, including Rosebud. She didn't like dancing for drunks for a living, but some nights she could bring home three hundred bucks just in tips. She couldn't make that kind of money anywhere else. And she needed that kind of money. She needed to keep Baxter in a good school, in a decent apartment, in a nice part of town. There was nothing she wouldn't do for her son. Nothing.

And she wouldn't do this forever. Just until something better came along. As far as she was concerned, it was a symptom of a sick society, though, when a classically trained dancer had to take her clothes off to make a living at her art.

She walked beyond the stage, into the back part of the building, which housed a communal dressing room for the dancers, the boss's office and the time clock, mounted on the wall in the hallway. Muffled voices came from Leo's office. If she wasn't quiet, he would be sure to come out and try to strong-arm her into working on her only night off. It never failed. So she walked softly up to the time clock in the hall. Sure enough, she spotted her check in the slot with her time card. Rosebud's was in her slot, as well. "Damn Leo Hardison," she muttered under her breath. He couldn't be bothered to stick them into an envelope and mail them. She snatched both checks up, then tiptoed into the dressing room and spotted Rosebud's denim bag slung over the back of a chair near her makeup mirror. She'd half turned to go when something caught her eye, made her turn back. On Rosebud's dressing table a fat manilla envelope sat in front of the makeup mirror. The name Jenny Lee Walker was typed across the front.

Frowning, Jasmine picked it up and murmured, "That's funny. I didn't think anybody but me knew

Rosebud's real name." It was addressed to her in care of The Catwalk; the return address was some law firm in Texas. Vaguely, Jasmine thought of the lawyer who'd contacted Rosebud with the news of her mother's death. Must be connected. Hell, maybe Rosebud had inherited a fortune or something. Jasmine stuffed the two checks and the big envelope inside Rosebud's oversize denim bag, hitched it over her shoulder and turned to leave.

She walked quietly into the hall and started down it, intending to go past Leo's office to the back door, which would save her a few steps. His office door was closed anyway, and the back door would open from the inside, even when the lock was engaged.

She was almost to the back exit when the gunshots rang out. Three explosions, equally spaced, each one making her heart slam against her chest and her entire body jerk in reaction as she stood there frozen. *Bang. Bang. Bang.*

Leo's office door flew open ahead of her, and she could see, for just an instant, very clearly inside. Leo stood there, holding the door open but still facing inside, muttering, "What the hell did you do? Dammit, Petronella, what the hell did you do?"

Another man, familiar to her from the club, stood over the still body of a third, his back to Jasmine. "Did what I had to."

Jasmine's horrified gaze slid down to the man on the floor. He was bleeding from his head, a dark pool that spread itself slowly underneath him. Then something made her look past the body, up at the rear window. She saw the wide eyes and wire-rimmed glasses of her little boy looking right back at her.

"He was a cop!" Leo said. "You've murdered a freaking cop!"

Jasmine had to move, and she had to move fast, before either of those men looked up and saw Baxter there. She couldn't get out the back door without moving right past Leo's open office door, so she backed away instead, inching, as silently as her shaking knees would allow, back up the hall. If Leo or that other man so much as turned their heads, they would see Baxter.

"Why the hell didn't you know about this before now? Huh? What the hell am I paying you for, anyway?" Leo demanded, his voice loud, ringing, bouncing off the walls of the empty bar and off the insides of her head.

The other man swore. "I don't know everything that happens in the department, Leo. What do you think I am, the chief or something? Besides, this guy wasn't one of mine. He was a Fed."

A federal agent, her mind whispered, but only briefly. She didn't have time to listen or to try to analyze their words. She had to get to Baxter. Get him out of here before either Leo or his murdering cohort saw him...or realized she had ever been here. She eased back up the hall, the way she'd

come, out into the front of the bar, toward the front
door. She opened it carefully, started outside. And
then she heard the clanging metal of those trash
cans out back, underneath Leo's window.

"What the hell was that?" Leo asked suddenly.

Jasmine ran. She raced around the club, to the
lot in the back. As she neared the lot, she saw Baxter running toward the car. The trash cans near the
window he'd been peering through were lying on
their sides. Then the bar's back door opened just as
Baxter reached the car and yanked the passenger
door open. Leo and the other man lunged out. The
killer, Petronella, had a gun, and he lifted it, pointed
it at Baxter, as the boy pulled the car door closed
behind him. A shot rang out.

"Leave him alone!" Jasmine scooped up a broken piece of brick and hurled it at the man for all
she was worth. It clocked him in the head, and he
went to his knees. She heard her car start up and
couldn't believe it. Leo was turning toward her
now, squinting and shielding his eyes. He was looking right into the sun, and she was in the shadow
of the building, she realized. But the other man was
struggling to his feet again, pulling up the gun,
pointing it at her. The next thing Jasmine knew, her
car was lurching forward. She had to jump out of
the way or get hit. Baxter's head was so low she
didn't think he could possibly see where he was
going. The car roared to a jerking, rocking stop
right between her and the killer, and she yanked the

door open and climbed in, shoving her baby aside, holding him down with one hand. She stomped the gas pedal and left rubber as she sped away.

"My God, baby. My God, baby, are you okay?" She kept her foot to the floor, veering in and out of lanes, as she ran her free hand over her son's head, his neck, his shoulders. "Are you hurt, Bax? Are you all right?" Her eyes were on him more than they were on the road, scanning him for injuries, fully expecting to see blood and bullet holes.

"I'm okay, Mom. I'm okay."

"You are?"

He nodded. Tears streaming, Jasmine let the relief course through her. It was true; he hadn't been hit. "Thank you, Jesus," she whispered, pulling him up onto the seat, into a one-armed hug. She kissed his face, felt the way he was trembling. She looked in the rearview mirror. No sign of anyone chasing them. She slowed down an iota. "Come on, baby, get your seat belt on now. We're gonna take you somewhere safe. Somewhere far, far away from those bad men. I promise you that. You're safe now, Baxter."

He nodded, but she didn't think he believed her.

Three things kept running through Jasmine's mind over and over again as she drove. Leo and that other man—the man she'd been seeing around The Catwalk for weeks lately—they'd seen her car. They'd seen Baxter. And they knew he had witnessed them murdering a federal agent. They'd tried

to kill her little boy, and it would not be difficult
for them to find her. She stroked Baxter's hair as
she drove, while he refused to shed a single tear
and yet shook all over. "It's gonna be okay, baby.
I promise, it's gonna be okay."

He wasn't talking, wasn't asking questions,
which was so unlike him that it scared her. His little
arms were twined tight around his waist, his head
down, his whole body shaking. Every few seconds
Jasmine glanced into her rearview mirror again, but
she didn't see them following her.

No, they wouldn't follow her. Why the hell
should they? They knew where she lived.

Suddenly her heart seemed to freeze in her chest.
Rosebud! God, she had to warn Rosebud! Looking
around her, she spotted a pay phone. Dammit, she
was so afraid to stop the car. But she had to.

She circled the block three times. The phone was
on a corner, near a convenience store. It was broad
daylight. It shouldn't feel so damn frightening.
"Mama's gotta make a phone call, honey," she
said softly, finally pulling the car to a stop with the
driver's door right beside the pay phone. "Scootch
right over here behind the wheel, baby. You can
hold my hand the whole time, okay?"

Nodding, his huge dark eyes riveted to hers and
wet with unshed tears, Baxter gripped her hand. She
opened the car door, the quarter already in her hand.
Getting out, she kept hold of Baxter with the other
hand and dropped the coin into the slot. Carefully

she punched the numbers. She noticed her nails. She and Rosebud had both had their nails freshly done just yesterday. Extra long and curving, and ruby-red. Rosebud had a white rose painted on every nail. Jasmine had opted for tiny sparkling bits of glass that looked like diamonds. They gleamed in the sunlight now as she punched the numbers on the keypad. Then she listened while the phone in her apartment rang and rang and rang. Why didn't she answer? Rosebud would have turned on the answering machine if she'd gone out.

What was she supposed to do, dammit? What the hell was she going to do?

She put the phone down, slid back into the car with Baxter, closed the door. *Think. Think, dammit!*

Rosebud might be out on the stoop. She did that sometimes, just sat on the stoop and watched the people go by. Said it helped her think. Jasmine could just drive by. Just drive by, not stop, not go inside, not risk her baby. Just drive by and see. If Rosebud was there, she could pick her up and they would be out of there. That would work. She could see it all plainly in her mind. She would just pick Rosebud up and they would speed away. And everything would be fine. They could go to some other city. It could work. She was forty-five minutes from the apartment by now. God, please let her get back in time.

She drove as fast as she dared. And when she got to her neighborhood, she put on her sunglasses and skirted the outermost streets, then dared to get in closer. "Lie down on the floor, baby," she told Baxter. "Stay down low for just a minute, okay, honey?"

He didn't argue, didn't ask why, for once. He just did what she said. She almost sobbed in a mix of relief and worry. It wasn't like her Bax to be so timid, so obedient, so quiet.

She turned and went closer, not turning onto her own street but passing by it and glancing down it as she did.

"Oh, no..."

Lights, flashing red and blue. Lots of them. She could see people standing in the street. She turned the wheel, went around the block, came back up to her street on the other side—her building was on the corner. She could see clearly from this end. She drove, almost holding her breath, until she reached the corner. And then she stopped and just sat there and looked.

Two men carried a stretcher out the front door onto the stoop, and started down the steps to the waiting ambulance. But the person on that stretcher didn't need any ambulance. Jasmine could see, even from here, the black vinyl that enveloped the victim on that stretcher. A body bag.

The men paused on the top step as a uniformed officer spoke to them. Leaning over, he unzipped the vinyl tomb. A hand fell free, slender and white, and Jasmine sucked in a breath. Long, freshly done nails adorned that hand. Bright red, with something tiny and white on every one.

She clapped a hand over her mouth to keep from crying out loud. But her tears rolled so thick and so fast she couldn't stop them.

Behind her, a horn blasted. She was holding up traffic.

The cop paused in zipping the body back up again and turned to look her way. Jasmine froze as she got a full view of his face. He was the same man who'd been with Leo this morning—the same man who'd killed a federal agent and done his best to kill her, too. He stood there with the sun winking off his shiny badge, and Jasmine whispered, "Petronella."

His eyes narrowed on her, and he lifted a hand to shield them from the sun, as if trying to see better. Jasmine stomped on the gas pedal, and the car lurched away.

Chapter 3

Luke kicked a chunk of moss off the wide stone steps of the old brick house and gnawed his lower lip. "I've made up my mind, Garrett," he said to his cousin, a man who, in the past three months, had become almost a brother to him, something that still amazed Luke to no end. "I'm staying."

He looked up, saw the wide grin he'd known damn well he would see on the big man's Stetson-shaded face. Garrett slapped his shoulder. "The family's gonna be glad to hear that, Luke. Chelsea's been nagging me every single night on this one. 'Can't you talk him into staying? Why don't you try harder?' And so on and on and on."

Luke blew a long sigh. "I didn't mean to leave everyone hanging so long. It's just that, well, it wasn't an easy decision." He looked at the gleaming machine parked in the long driveway. "That rig's been my partner and pretty much my only friend for a long while now. But...well, hell, Garrett, I guess it took Buck's dying to make me realize it wasn't the only thing I wanted out of life."

Garrett nodded. Luke had talked to him at length about Buck's life and death, and that moment when he'd made the decision to come out here. So he knew the story. "Does that mean you've figured out what you do want, Luke?"

Luke smiled. "What I've figured out is that my options are wide-open. I loved my mother dearly, Garrett, but she did me a little bit of a disservice in raising me the way she did. Refusing to share me with anyone else, or to let anyone else get close to her—to either of us. She raised me to believe it was better to be closed off, independent, solitary." He shook his head. "I never in my wildest dreams imagined being a part of a huge, sprawling family like this one."

Garrett nodded. "I can't imagine not being a part of it. And it seems to just keep getting bigger!"

Luke laughed aloud, thinking of the two expectant daddies in the clan, Wes and Elliot, and how close Taylor and Esmeralda were to their due dates.

"But that's the beauty of it, Garrett. And that's what I want. I've spent a lot of time figuring that out. So much that I can see it in my mind just as clear as I can see you standing there. I want what you have, Garrett. I want a home that opens its arms up to me when I walk in the front door.'' He turned and looked back at the still sad looking brick house, seeing only its potential. ''I want a family that does the same. I want to find a woman who wants the same things out of life that I do. A good, clean, wholesome woman who can make biscuits and babies.''

Garrett laughed out loud, a deep booming sound. ''Well, we got the home part covered, at least. This place goes up for auction next week. And you're the only interested party in town.''

''How do you know that?'' Luke asked.

''My wholesome wife, my wholesome sister, my wholesome sisters-in-law—they're not beneath snooping. And it's a small town, so snooping ain't all that difficult. If anyone else were planning to bid on this old place at that tax auction, we'd know about it by now. They aren't.''

Sighing deeply, Luke looked at his rig, all shine and polish, in the dirt driveway. She gleamed under the bright Texas sunshine like a gem in a spotlight. ''Hell, I can't say I won't miss her,'' he said. ''But I got a hell of an offer on her.''

''You gonna take it?''

''Already did,'' Luke said. ''The buyer will be here this afternoon to pick her up. He's paying me enough to buy this place outright.''

''It'll take a lot of fixing up, you know.'' Garrett

gripped the old iron railing on the flagstone steps, gave it a shake. It wobbled loosely back and forth.

"Like I could have rented this place for three months and not figured that one out?"

Garrett shrugged. "It's solid, though, at the heart of it. Just needs some surface work done."

"Of course it's solid—it's made of brick. This is the one that even the Big Bad Wolf couldn't blow down." He slid his gaze over the faded red brick, the thick green vines twisting up the sides, with huge pink blossoms trumpeting every few inches. Both floors were lined with arched, stone-silled windows, the bricks around them turned lengthwise in fancy fan patterns. "They don't build them like this anymore."

"And don't forget the best part," Garrett said. "It's right next door to the Texas Brand."

"Key selling point," Luke said, and they both laughed.

Garrett's smile faded, and a sincere expression took its place. "I'm glad you came to us, Luke. And even more glad that you're staying."

Lowering his head, Luke shook it slowly. "You all made me feel like family right from the first. That's something I've never had. Never thought I could have."

"You *are* family. Don't forget that. In a family where family comes first, that means a whole lot." Garrett grinned. "Now I'm gonna head home before I wax any more sappy than I already have. See you for dinner, right?''

"Depends. Whose turn is it to cook?"

"Mine," Garrett said. "I'm barbequing ribs. You don't want to miss that."

"Trust me, I won't."

Garrett smiled from ear to ear and turned to go, his long strides eating up the distance to his oversize pickup nearby.

Luke stood there a moment on the porch of his new home, the place where he'd come to find his roots, to start over, to make something of his own. He walked slowly to the rig, where she sat in the driveway. "Well, old girl, I guess this is just about it. We've come to a fork in the road. You're goin' one way, and I'm goin' the other." He took off his duck-billed bulldog hat, opened the truck door and gently set it on the seat. Closing the door again, he headed back to the house, up the stone stairway, across the porch. He took another hat from the rack just inside the door. The Stetson of dark brown felt, with the leather hatband around it. He put it on.

He'd been switching hats for a while now. One day thinking of staying here and wearing the cowboy hat. The next day, aching for the open road and wearing his Mack hat. But today he knew he'd made a decision. He adjusted the Stetson on his head. And it felt right.

"This is it, baby," Jasmine said softly.

Baxter stirred beside her. He'd fallen asleep

miles and miles ago. For a while Jasmine hadn't been at all sure that she would ever find this place, tucked out here in the middle of nowhere. But now she knew she had. She looked at the photo that had been in the package addressed to Jenny Lee Walker. Her beautiful, gentle Rosebud. The big old brick house her headlights picked out of the dark Texas night was identical, right down to the vines clinging to one side. And the directions the lawyer had included in the package had been pretty close, too. She'd only gotten lost twice.

Rosebud's mother had left her this place. And Rosebud had no one else but Jasmine. She had been like a sister to Jasmine—like a second mom to Baxter, and Jasmine knew Rosebud had loved them as much as she could love anyone. She would have wanted it this way. And with the way things had happened—well, it almost seemed predestined. Rosebud was dead. Jasmine was on the run with Rosebud's bag—her ID, credit cards and driver's license—and that big envelope from the lawyer containing directions to the old house that belonged to Rosebud now, all in her back seat. Well, with all of that, it was easy to believe that maybe this was the way it was supposed to happen. It seemed way beyond the realm of coincidence.

At any rate, she was here now. At Rosebud's house. Jenny Lee's. She had to remember to call herself Jenny Lee. This wasn't Chicago. It wasn't a city, and the women here didn't use stage names. A Jenny Lee could blend in here, hide for a while in this haven while she decided what to do. A Rosebud would stand out.

She shut the car off in the driveway and removed the keys. The headlights went out, plunging the house into darkness. God, it was dark here. A thousand stars dotted the sky, but there was no moon tonight. Not a streetlight to be found. Jasmine opened the car door and heard the chirping, humming insects. She took a breath and smelled the sweetest smell on the wind. Flowers, maybe the ones on those vines that clung to the house.

Dark here, she mused, wasn't as scary as dark in Chicago. Dark here smelled good, and it had a musical backup that didn't include honking horns and screaming sirens. She was overcome suddenly with the feeling that she had done the right thing. Baxter would be safe here.

She shouldered Rosebud's bag—her bag now—scooped her sleepy son up into her arms and pushed the car door closed with her hip. "Look, baby," she said softly. "See this nice house? Hmm? It's far, far away from everything bad, Baxter. It's safe here. And it's just gonna be you and me from here on in. No one will ever hurt you, or scare you like that ever again. Okay?"

"But...but, Mom, whose house is this?" He tugged his glasses from his shirt pocket and put them on.

She sniffed. "It's your Aunt Rosebud's, baby. She only found out about it the other day. She wants us to stay here, to be safe."

"So those bad men won't find us?" he asked.

"Yes."

He nodded, squirmed out of her arms and stood on his feet, holding her hand in one of his, rubbing his eyes with the other. Jasmine started forward. Baxter planted his feet.

"What is it, baby?" she asked, looking down at him.

"Are you sure they can't find us here?"

He looked up at her, so trusting, so frightened. "I'm sure, Baxter."

"They found Aunt Rosebud, didn't they, Mom?"

She closed her eyes.

"I saw," Baxter said softly. "You told me to stay down on the floor, but I didn't, Mom. I saw those men taking somebody away in an ambulance. It was Aunt Rosebud, wasn't it? That's why we didn't go pick her up and bring her with us...isn't it, Mom?"

Sniffling, Jasmine nodded. "Yeah, baby. But I don't want you to worry about your Aunt Rosebud anymore. She's with the angels now."

Baxter looked at the sky. A giant tear rolled down his face, from beneath his glasses, over his cheek. "I'm gonna miss you, Aunt Rosebud."

Closing her eyes to prevent her own tears from

spilling over, Jasmine scooped Bax up again, into her arms. He wrapped his legs around her waist and his arms around her neck like a little spider monkey, and she carried him across the worn driveway and up the wide flagstone steps to the porch. There had been a key in that packet from the lawyer. She held the key in her hand now. But when she braced the screen open with her hip and gripped the doorknob with a free hand, she found it turned freely. The place wasn't even locked.

That was odd.

She pushed the door open and stepped inside, into darkness. Her hands groped for a light switch. She really didn't expect much of a result when she snapped it on. But the room flooded with light anyway.

Blinking, she looked around, not understanding what she was seeing. The place was clean, neat, furnished. A brick fireplace faced her like a centerpiece, a few items resting on its stone hearth. A tacky red ceramic bull. A silver candle holder with no candles in it. A framed photograph of a semi truck. What the hell? To the left a huge archway led to another room, and a dark stairway led to the second floor. To the right were tall narrow windows, hung with dark green drapes. The furniture was mismatched. An overstuffed chair with a leafy green print. A dark brown corduroy recliner that listed a bit to the right. A blue floral camel back sofa with what looked like a wool horse blanket thrown over the back. The blanket was striped, brown, black, gray and white, with fringe on the ends. A big oval braided rug covered most of the floor, but she could see the hardwood underneath around the edges. There was an odd-shaped coffee table that looked like a slice straight out of a giant redwood, with legs attached. The thing gleamed under layers of shellac and still had bark around the outer edges. And on that table was a coffee cup. With a tiny bit of dark brew still in the bottom. She turned to look back at the door she'd just entered. A cowboy hat hung from a peg beside it.

Okay. Okay, so maybe she should have read all the papers in that envelope of Rosebud's before heading down here. But damn, she'd been driving for two days, almost nonstop. And there had been sheaves of documents in that envelope. There just hadn't been time. She'd wanted to get away, far away, from men who fired guns at innocent little boys.

She shouldn't have expected it to be easy.

"I'm so tired, Mom."

Sighing, she hugged Baxter tight, then laid him down on the sofa and pulled the striped blanket over him. "You go on to sleep now, Bax. Everything's gonna be just fine. You'll see. Just go to sleep."

He closed his eyes and rolled onto his side, snuggling under the covers. Jasmine pulled off his glasses and set them on the coffee table. She stayed beside Baxter, stroking his head gently, until he was sound asleep. Then, with a sigh, she got up, went to the door and turned the locks. She checked every window in the living room, making sure their locks were fastened, as well.

Someone was living here. No doubt about that. But whoever it was, they were obviously not home right now. The place was pitch-dark, and no vehicle had been in the driveway. Maybe by the time they got back she would have figured out exactly what Rosebud's legal rights were here.

She took the shoulder bag, her smaller handbag tucked deep inside it, and stepped through the archway. Finding a light switch, she flicked it on and stared into a giant of a room. A counter separated the dining room part from the kitchen part. She spotted the back door at the far end of the kitchen, made sure it was locked, and checked the windows in this portion of the house, as well. And then, finally feeling relatively safe, she hauled the big envelope out of Rosebud's bag and emptied its contents onto the table. She needed to figure out exactly what the situation was here. She'd expected to find an empty, abandoned house awaiting her, not one that was obviously being lived in. Rosebud's mother had been in a nursing home for the past two years, as far as Jasmine knew. So who'd been staying in her house? Thank goodness, she'd arrived while they were away. At least she'd caught one lucky break.

Her eyes felt dry and heavy as she sat at the dining room table and started reading through the documents in front of her. She wondered vaguely if whoever had been here had left any of that coffee around and decided to find out.

Luke heard something downstairs but dismissed it, rolled over and tried to go back to sleep. He still wasn't used to sleeping in a big bed in the middle of an even bigger bedroom. He'd thought his sleeper unit had plenty of room. But even with the double king-size model, it had been like a closet compared to this. So much space around him. Hell, he'd barely slept at all for the first few weeks. And he hadn't been used to the noise, either. Oh, he heard noises all night long when he slept in his rig off an exit or in a rest area. But not these kinds of noises. He was used to horns, traffic, slamming doors, radios blasting. The noises out here were different. Crickets singing nonstop. Night birds calling soft and sad. Coyotes crying like they'd lost their best friend. The wind moaning sometimes, as it moved on past. The house creaking.

It smelled different here, too. Instead of diesel fumes and the exhaust of truck-stop fryers, the scent of honeysuckle drifted through the open window on a breeze, mingling with the sweet smells of lush meadow grasses and wildflowers.

And fresh-brewed coffee.

Luke's eyes opened wide. Coffee? Wait a minute, that wasn't right.

He came more fully awake and sniffed the air. Yes, that was definitely a coffee aroma floating up the stairs to tickle his senses. Sitting up slowly, frowning, he glanced at the glowing green numbers on his bedside clock and wondered who the heck would have come creeping into his house at three in the morning to make coffee.

One of his cousins, he thought, flinging back the covers. Maybe someone was in some kind of trouble. Wait a minute! Maybe one of the babies was coming! Wes's wife, Taylor, was expecting her first baby any day now, as was Esmeralda, Elliot's strange young bride. Maybe one of the newest members of his long-lost family was in the process of arriving!

Luke got to his feet with a little surge of excitement building in his chest. He pulled on his jeans and thrust his arms into the long sleeves of a western shirt he didn't bother snapping up. Barefoot, he headed down the stairs of the home that would be his the second the formality of the auction was over, a week from now.

Light spilled from the dining room, so he stepped out there, then he blinked and rubbed his eyes and looked again.

A woman was standing at his counter, her back to him, pouring freshly brewed coffee into his favorite mug. She had big hair. Big black glossy hair that fell in riots of curls clear to the middle of her back. She wore skintight leggings that hugged her round butt so tightly that it looked as if she wore a thin coat of black paint instead of pants. They were just as tight down her thighs, and then down to the spike-heeled boots on her feet. There was an inch of toned flesh between where the pants ended and where the shirt began—if it could be called a shirt. It was made of metallic mesh so he could see right through to the bra or whatever she wore underneath. Right now it was merely a thin black strip across her back, beneath the silver mesh of the blouse.

"Excuse me?" he said, when he could find his voice.

The woman whirled so fast her coffee sloshed over the sides of the cup and her big dangling earrings jangled like bells. Her eyes were as wide as saucers—huge dark eyes, lined in black, darkly shadowed lashes so thick they had to be fake. Lips so plump and red they looked like juicy ripe berries. He didn't think he'd ever seen so much makeup on one face before—'cept maybe on the dancing girls in Vegas. She didn't say anything, just took a step backward and reached for something. He heard rattling

"Didn't mean to startle you, ma'am." He held up both hands, starting toward her. "I mean, I'm not gonna call the police or anything. Just curious as to what you're doing in my house in the middle of the night. Besides making coffee, I mean." He moved still closer.

She lifted a butcher knife. He saw it, went still and noticed her long, long nails, the bright red polish and the little glittery stones affixed to each one. "You're, uh...not from around here, are you?" he asked her.

"Who are you?" she asked him. "What do you want?"

"What do *I* want?" He shook his head, his humor fading fast. "Put the knife down."

She only lifted it higher.

"Okay, fine, I'll start. And I'll talk over the knife." He glanced sideways at the phone. Wondered what his chances were of dialing Garrett's place before she could sink that blade into his back deep enough to kill him. Wondered why the hell she would want to. "I'm Luke Brand. And this is my place."

She shook her head fast. "You're lying. Rosebu—my mother left me this house in her will. It's mine, not yours, and I want to know what you're doing trespassing."

"Whoa, whoa, just a minute. Okay, it isn't my place...yet. But I do live here." He followed her gaze to the papers strewn all over the table. "You see, this place is about to be auctioned for back taxes. You've made some kind of mistake. Now, I'm not gonna hold a grudge. You just put the knife down and gather up your papers and be on your way."

"I'm not going anywhere."

He took another step toward her, and she brandished the knife, slashing with it, though he was pretty sure she didn't have any intention of cutting him. Still, it pissed him off. "Hell, that's about all of that I can take," he said. His hand shot out, capturing hers at the wrist. She punched him in the belly with her free hand, so he snapped his arm around her waist and pulled her hard against him, holding her empty arm pinned between his body and hers. Her knife-wielding hand was still in his grip.

She stared up at him, wide-eyed, panting. "Let me go," she whispered.

He stared right back down at her. "Drop the knife."

"Never."

Luke shrugged. "Fine. I can hold you like this all night." But the words made him uncomfortably aware of her body there against his. Firm, tight little body, he thought. She felt like an athlete in his arms.

"Drop the knife," he said again.

"Go to hell," she replied.

Chapter 4

The man was long and tall and hard all over. Lean, and strong. Not soft and fleshy like the men she was used to fending off after hours at The Catwalk. She wouldn't be able to best him in a fight. But she wasn't going to surrender her only weapon, either, leaving Baxter defenseless in the next room.

The man held her for a long time. He was warm and clean. He smelled like the air here. Fresh and sweet, but with a subtle musky scent underlying all that—man scent. With his shirt open and his chest bare, it would be impossible not to notice. Especially since, at the moment, he was holding her pretty firmly against that bare chest. Her nose was almost touching it, her lips only a breath away.

Finally, with a sigh, he said, "I'm gonna be mad as hell if you slice me with my own knife, lady."

"I won't cut you unless you give me reason," she said.

"I won't give you reason. Hell, I *like* women."

She swallowed hard, certain he was up to something. "How stupid would I have to be to put the knife down?" she said. "I'm a woman, alone in the house with a man I don't know. So just let me go."

He seemed to think on that for a moment. "You know, you have a point there. Although it's a twisted one, being that you're the one who broke into *my* house—"

"I didn't break in. It was open. And if it hadn't been, I'd have used my key. Which I have—because it's *my* house."

He sighed, gnawed his lip. His heat was seeping through her clothes now, and this was way too close to be held to a man she'd never met. Way too close. And feeling way too little like a threat and too much like an embrace. Stupid, yes. But he wasn't hurting her. And she wasn't struggling to pull free.

"Okay, I'm gonna let you go now," he said at last. "I'll just take a step backward and let you go, and then you can explain to me what's going on here, okay?"

Her eyes affixed to his, she nodded slowly, every muscle coiled and ready for action. If he so much as looked like he might try anything...

He let go of her waist first, stepping back, away from her, before he released her wrist.

She lowered her arm, still clutching the knife to

her side. He drew a breath, watching her. It occurred to her that he seemed as wary and suspicious of her as she was of him. Never taking his eyes off the knife, he spoke, as carefully and softly as if he were speaking to a wild animal. "You say your mother left you this place in her will."

She nodded toward the table. "I got that package from her lawyer the day before yesterday. See for yourself."

He glanced quickly at the papers strewn on the table. "Do, um, you mind if I get a cup of that coffee first?"

She narrowed her eyes on him. "Sit. I'll get it."

He lifted his brows. "Either you're overcome with the irresistible urge to wait on me or you don't want me near the knife drawer," he said, but he kept his tone light, even attempted a shaky smile. She didn't respond, and his smile died. "Fine. I'll sit."

She kept the man in her peripheral vision as he went to the table, sat down and began to sort through the paperwork. But he was still nervous. He would look at the papers, then at her, back and forth, rapidly. He was probably afraid she would slip up behind him and slide her blade into his back. She was almost enjoying being the one in a position of power over him. It wasn't often she had the upper hand with a man. She poured him coffee, and picked up her own mug, carrying both in one hand, the knife in the other. She set his cup down, then took the seat opposite him.

"So, uh…you're Jenny Lee Walker?" he asked.

"Yes."

He held her gaze for a moment. Pursed his lips.

"What?"

"Nothing. You just…don't exactly look like a Jenny Lee to me."

Hell, neither had the real one, she thought. Aloud she said, "People change. I haven't used the name in years."

"No? What name have you been using?"

She could have said Rosebud. But sticking as close to the truth as possible had its benefits. It would only confuse Baxter to hear this man call her Rosebud. "Jasmine," she said finally.

He blinked. "Jasmine? Really?"

"What's wrong with Jasmine?" she asked, instantly defensive.

He shrugged. "Nothing. It…uh…it was my mother's favorite flower is all." He sighed and glanced at the papers again. "Well, Jasmine, your mother made this will over two years ago. According to the pages from the lawyer, Buzz Montana—he's local, by the way, so you can talk to him yourself if you want to—he's been renting the land out to defray the expenses of keeping it up and to cover his own fees. In fact, I know the ranchers who've been using the land to graze their cattle. Apparently things got bad enough that he decided to rent the house, as well. That was about the time I came along looking for a place. But it still wasn't enough to pay the taxes.''

She blinked. ''Taxes?''

''Property taxes. Look, this lawyer, he's been looking for you for two years. Where have you been?''

''That's none of your business,'' she said sharply. ''I'm here now. And the place is mine.''

''Not if you can't pay the back taxes, it's not. The state's going to auction the place off to get their money.''

''Then it's mine until they do. It hasn't been sold yet, has it?''

''No. Not until a week from now. But—''

''Then for a week it's mine.'' And that, she told herself, would be long enough to figure out what the hell to do next.

He rose from his chair very slowly. ''Look, lady, I don't even know if you *are* Jenny Lee Walker. For all I know you could have mugged her and stolen this envelope, along with her wallet.''

She lifted her brows, getting to her feet, as well. ''Oh, so I look like a mugger to you?''

''Or worse.''

Her jaw dropped. She blinked in shock, because the slam was so unexpected. ''What's that supposed to mean?''

''It means that I didn't fall off the turnip truck yesterday, honey. I've seen a lot of women like you in a lot of truck stops around this country. They come knocking on the sleeper in the middle of the night, asking if you want your *windows washed*."

"You think I'm a whore?"

He shrugged. "You sure as hell look like one."

She smacked him. Hard, right across the face, and her long nails dragged over his cheek, leaving marks. Then they stood there, facing off across the table. She wasn't usually violent, but she'd been through hell the past two days. She'd seen a murder. She'd dodged bullets and seen them narrowly miss her little boy. She'd lost her best friend when she had been the real target. And she'd driven for hours and hours almost nonstop. She was tired, hungry and scared to death, and just when she had finally found what was supposed to be a haven, this redneck had to rise up and get in her way.

He stood there, not rocked in the least, it seemed, by the blow, even though tiny red beads were appearing now on his cheek.

"If you think you're gonna walk in here in the middle of the night," he said, "and throw me out of my own house—"

"*My* own house," she corrected.

"Tell you what. You show me proof you're Jenny Lee Walker and I'll let you stay."

"I don't have to prove anything to you. Who the hell do you think you are, anyway? I *own* this place. I don't have to answer to you. You're the one trespassing here."

"I've paid my rent for the month," he snapped. "And I *can* prove that. You couldn't throw me out if you wanted to."

"Oh, trust me, I want to."

"Well, it ain't gonna happen. The only person being thrown out of here is you, lady. Now. Bag and baggage." He looked around. "Where is your baggage, anyway?"

"Still in the car," she lied. She couldn't very well tell him she'd arrived without much besides the clothes on her back, could she? He already suspected too much.

"Good. That should make this easier." He reached for her arm, closed his hand around it. "I don't want your kind hanging around here. So let's go. Come on."

"Mommy?"

The man's face changed. His smug, cynical sneer vanished. He looked as if he'd just been hit between the eyes with a sizable hammer.

Jasmine snapped her head to the left and saw Baxter standing in that big open archway, the blanket from the sofa wrapped around him and trailing behind. He'd gotten up and put his glasses on. She jerked her arm free of the stranger's grip and went to Baxter, knelt in front of him. "Oh, baby, I'm so sorry I woke you up with all that noise. It's okay, honey, I promise. It's okay." She hugged him.

He was looking past her, though, at the man. She sensed it the way mothers sense so many things about their sons. And she felt his fear, too. "Is he one of the bad men, Mommy? Is he one of the—"

"Hush, baby. Hush, it's all right." She held her boy closer, praying he would say no more. She didn't need this stranger knowing her business.

She heard the stranger's voice as he muttered something under his breath. She thought he was cussing softly, but she couldn't really hear enough to be sure. Then his footsteps, soft and nearly soundless on the floor. And the next thing she heard was his voice again, coming from closer than before—and in a totally different tone.

"Hey there, kiddo," he said. "My name's Luke Brand. What's yours?"

"B-Baxter."

Jasmine straightened, picking Bax up, holding him tight to her and turning to put his back to the man, but Baxter twisted in her arms to face him anyway.

"Well, Baxter, I don't know what...what bad men you're talking about—" he slanted a brief glance at Jasmine "—but I promise, I'm not one of them. We don't allow bad men out here."

"You don't?"

"Nope. Cross my heart. Your mom and I were just trying to straighten out some mix-ups, that's all."

"Oh." Baxter looked at Jasmine. "Do we really have to leave, Mom? It's still dark outside, and I'm scared. I don't want to go back out there. And we've been in the car for such a long time already, and—"

"Nobody has to go anywhere tonight," Luke Brand said softly. He met Jasmine's eyes, held them this time. "And there's nothing to be afraid of. Not around here." He reached out and tousled Baxter's thick, dark blond hair. "Okay, Baxter?"

Baxter smiled and laid his head on his mother's shoulder. "Okay," he said.

Jasmine watched the man for signs of a con, but he seemed perfectly sincere, which was, of course, ridiculous. He was after something. He had an angle. She just hadn't spotted it yet. She would have expected him to be twice as eager to be rid of her once he realized she had a kid in tow. Most men were. Instead, he'd changed his attitude entirely. The hostility had vanished. And this Mr. Nice Guy routine had fallen into its place.

"Top of the stairs, Jasmine. First door on the left. That's the only bedroom made up for actual use at the moment. You and Baxter go on up there and get some rest. We can figure the rest of this out in the morning."

His bed? He was giving her *his bed?*

She licked her lips, lowered her head, but didn't say thanks. She held Baxter a little tighter, snatched up her shoulder bag, turned and headed up the stairs without a backward glance.

Luke watched the woman go up the stairs and stood there for a long moment after she was out of sight. Hell. He felt as if he'd just been awakened by a hurricane that had only just blown itself out. Or maybe he was in the eye, because she would sure as hell be ripping and roaring in the morning.

The woman was a puzzle. Small and sexy as they made them. She had a centerfold's body and dressed to show it. Tight, tiny clothes. Too much makeup. Talons that would make a bald eagle jealous. Big, *big* hair. And she'd been packing so much heavy metal that she jingled and jangled with every move. Necklaces, bracelets, no less than a half-dozen pairs of little earrings to complement the big ones. No other piercings though. None visible, anyway. That didn't mean they weren't there.

He'd thought he had her pegged.

Then he'd heard that little voice calling her Mommy, and his theory got blown to hell. Oh, maybe it could have held its own if she'd reacted to that plea with a scowl, or by snapping at the kid. But no. Her face had gone all achy. Like that little voice calling her name was all it took to break her heart to bits. Her eyes even welled up. And then the way she picked the boy up and held him so protectively. She'd looked fierce then. Like she would claw Luke's eyes out if he so much as looked at the kid wrong.

That look was the one that got to him. Because *that* look was one he knew too well to ever mistake it. He'd seen it far too often—in his own mother's

eyes. That fierce, single-minded devotion, the pro-
tectiveness that warned outsiders to stay clear.
Luke's mother had loved him like that. Because he
was all she'd had. Hell, she had almost ruined him
with that fiercely protective love.

Jenny Lee—if that was her real name—loved her
son utterly. That had been obvious to Luke in the
few moments he'd seen them together. And any
woman capable of loving a child that much,
well...she rose a notch in his book. Hooker or no,
she couldn't be all bad. Whether she loved him too
much—enough to damage the kid—well, that remained to be seen.

The little boy, now there was another puzzle. Because that kid had been scared. No two ways about
it. And who were these "bad men" he'd been
afraid of?

Of course, no matter how devoted a mother Jasmine was or how frightened a child Baxter was, one
truth remained that made them both Luke's enemies, in a manner of speaking. They had come to
lay claim to the home he was in the process of
making his own. They had come to derail his new
start. They had come to take away the only thing
he'd ever wanted badly enough to give up his rig
for. He had sold his prize possession for this place.
That couldn't be undone. There was no way he
would give up without a hell of a fight.

Luke sat down, drank his coffee and pondered on
the two wanderers for a while, giving them plenty

of time to fall asleep as he continued to peruse the legal papers on the table. Then he slipped outside to the car. It was a ten-year-old station wagon, with plenty of rust. She'd locked it, of course, and the key was more than likely tucked into that oversize shoulder bag she'd taken to bed with her. But it was a car that had no trunk, so he figured if there was any luggage to be seen, he'd see it. Only he didn't. Because there wasn't any. It seemed to him that the woman had come here with nothing more than the clothes on her back and whatever she'd managed to cram into that shoulder bag of hers, which couldn't be much.

Illinois plates. She'd come a long way, then. He made a note of the number. Garrett could easily check it out. Having a cousin who was a small-town sheriff could, he realized, come in handy. He peered through the glass of the driver's door. He saw empty pop bottles and fast-food wrappers. Every one of them from some kind of "kid's meal." They'd eaten on the road. Or Baxter had, at least. Hadn't the woman eaten at all?

Sighing, he went back inside, settled himself down at the dining room table and proceeded to read every remaining scrap of paper in the large envelope she'd brought with her. He read until his head ached and his eyes watered, but he still couldn't find the truth she was hiding. And it was obvious there was one.

Hell.

He waited till six o'clock to call Garrett, knowing his cousin's house would be bustling with life by then. Garrett liked to get up before his wife and make a pot of coffee. He would pour her a cup when he heard her coming down the stairs. Claimed it was best to do this silently, give the caffeine a chance to kick in and then attempt human conversation. Of course, that was just a cover. Chelsea was head over heels for the big guy. Garrett probably just liked to have those few quiet minutes in the morning with his wife all to himself before little Bubba had to get up for school and the real world came crashing in.

Hell, Luke hated to interrupt that intimate few minutes for his cousin, but he wanted to catch Garrett before he headed out to check on the cattle, then went off to work at the sheriff's office in town.

Garrett answered on the second ring. And his greeting was, "This had better be good."

"Sorry, Garrett," Luke said. "But it is. Damn good. Or maybe damn bad would be more accurate."

"What's wrong, Luke?"

Luke could hear the concern in Garrett's tone, and he could also hear Chelsea in the background, asking if Luke was all right and what was going on. He smiled at the sweetness of having this big family suddenly all over every little problem.

"Tell your wife I'm fine. I just had an unexpected visitor drop by last night."

"He's fine, Chelsea. Give me a minute." Then Garrett sighed. "Ah, she's rushed upstairs to pick up the extension," he told Luke.

A second later the soft click told Luke that Chelsea was on the other phone.

"Go ahead, Luke," she said. "Tell us what's up."

He liked Chelsea. She was one of those rare, special women a man was lucky to stumble upon once in a lifetime. Garrett must have done something awfully good to have found her and made her his own.

"Okay," he said at last. "Last night a woman showed up here with a little boy. She says this place is hers, and that she's here to claim it."

Garrett said, "What's her name? Where's she from?"

Chelsea said, "What does she look like? Is she married?"

Luke withstood the bombardment of questions fairly well, he thought. "Her name, she says, is Jenny Lee Walker, but she goes by Jasmine. The car she's driving has Illinois plates on it."

"Number?" Garrett asked.

"DX7-381," Luke replied, rattling off the number he'd committed to memory. "She showed up with nothing at all, as far as I can see, besides her son and the clothes they're wearing, and this packet of papers from the law offices of Buzz Montana giving her ownership of this property. As for what she looks like, Chelsea, she looks like a high-priced lot lizard, and no, I don't think she's married. I didn't see a ring, anyway."

"So that means you looked," Chelsea said. "But what's a lot lizard?"

"It's trucker slang for a truck-stop prostitute," Garrett said, his tone decidedly darker. "And it's not the kind of observation a Brand man makes about a lady."

"She's no lady, Garrett. She broke in here, and when I came downstairs to see what was going on, she pulled a knife on me."

Garrett waited, but Luke said no more. Garrett said, "Why did she pull the knife, Luke?"

Luke thought on that. "I don't know. I guess I scared her."

"And?"

He shrugged. "Well, she had her son with her. I suppose she thought I might be a threat to him."

"Well damn, Luke," Chelsea said. "Seems to me that shows courage, character and devotion. I mean, you're a pretty big fella for a woman to try to take on all alone, just to protect her son." Then her voice brightened. "How old is the boy? Bubba's age?"

Luke sighed. "Whose side are you guys on here, anyway?"

He could almost hear Garrett smile. "Don't you worry, Luke. Family comes first with the Brands. Always has. But honor is right up there with it, and the Cowboy Code is our way of life."

Luke made a face. "Oh, come on. There's a code? Why is this the first I'm hearing of it?"

"It's the first time you've broken it, cousin," Garrett said. "Being kind to women and children is at the top of the list."

Luke groaned. "I *was* kind."

"Not if she heard that 'lot lizard' comment, you weren't."

Luke thought about his comment last night about her clothes and her violent reaction. He still had the claw marks on his face. His cheek still stung. "Well, the fact that she's still here—sleeping in my bed, I might add—ought to indicate my extreme kindness." He swallowed. "So what's the penalty for breaking this code of yours, anyway?"

Garrett sighed. "Well, when Ben, Wes and Elliot were kids, I'd just kick their backsides. But I suppose you're a bit too old for that. Then again..."

"Come on, Garrett!"

Garrett laughed softly, a deep rumbling sound. "Relax, will you? We'll be over after breakfast, okay? We'll get this all sorted out."

Breakfast. The mention of it made Luke's stomach growl. He was starved. It also made him think of the junk-food boxes and bags he'd seen in the woman's car last night. He bet the kid hadn't had an honest meal in at least a couple of days. And his mother might not have eaten much at all.

"Luke?"

"What? Oh, yeah, after breakfast. I'll see you then. And thanks, Garrett, Chelsea."

"That's what family's for, Luke," Chelsea said.

Drawing a deep breath, Luke hung up the phone. Family. He was willing to bet that if the woman upstairs had any family at all besides her son, she wouldn't be here.

Hell. Looking at the poor little kid was like looking at a dim reflection of his own past.

Sighing, Luke went to the kitchen and opened the fridge to see what he could find for breakfast.

Chapter 5

She smelled something that tickled her senses and crept into her dreams. She was young again—eight or nine years old, at the most—and she was at her best friend Mary's house for a sleepover. First thing in the morning, Mary's mom made this huge breakfast. It was the smell of bacon cooking that woke young Jasmine that morning. And she lay there for a minute and thought how cool it must be to have a mom like Mary's. To wake up every morning to the smell of bacon cooking, or the sound of her humming softly in the kitchen.

At home, Jasmine woke to the smell of stale cigarette smoke and beer. Her own mom greeted her most mornings by groaning in hangover misery and telling her to get the hell out of her room. There was usually a strange man in her bed on those mornings. She didn't want to go home again after a sleepover with Mary. Or with Jeannette or with Valerie. She didn't want to wake up to overflowing ashtrays and half-filled beer glasses and spilled food and whatever man her mother had decided would be more important than her daughter this week. She didn't ever want to go home again. She lay there, at Mary's house, and she told herself that when she was a mom someday, she would be the kind of mom who made bacon in the mornings. She would never let anything ever be more important to her than her child. Especially not some strange man.

"Mommy?"

Jasmine opened her eyes slowly. She was lying on her back in a strange bed, and her little boy's smiling face hovered an inch above her own. "Smell that, Mommy? It smells just like home on Sundays!"

Jasmine blinked the haze from her brain, lifted her head and kissed Baxter's nose. "It does, doesn't it?" she asked, sniffing the air and smelling bacon and coffee and something sweet.

Baxter nodded hard, grinning, eyes wide. "Is it Sunday, Mom?"

"Nope. It's only Saturday."

He shrugged. "You think Mr. Brand is cooking us breakfast?"

"I don't know, honey."

"Can I go find out?"

''No, not just yet.'' She got out of the bed and looked down at herself. She'd slept in her clothes, minus the nylons and shoes, and they were wrinkled and messy. A glance in the mirror across the room almost made her jump. Her hair was wild and her makeup smeared. She looked like hell. She didn't want to face anyone like this.

The bedroom was nice, though. She'd come in here in the dark last night, and frankly, she'd been too tired to care to look around. She'd crawled into bed to snuggle with Bax until he fell asleep. The plan had been to get up and find a shower afterward, but she'd been out cold before she got around to it. She saw the bathroom now, as she looked around. It was just through a small door to the right, and a peek inside told her there were a tub and shower, towels and washcloths. Thank goodness.

She turned back to finish her inspection of the bedroom. The outmost wall was lined in tall narrow windows with sheer white curtains that let the sun beam through them like a golden spotlight. The bed was an old-looking four-poster, made of some dark, lustrous hardwood, and the large dresser matched. The bedside stand didn't. It was newer, and cheap looking, wood veneer, not the real stuff. And there was a small portable television set on top of the trunk at the foot of the bed. Not a picture on the wall. Not a rug on the floor. No trinkets or knick-nacks in sight. How long did that Luke character say he'd been living here? Three months? He sure didn't settle into a place fast, did he?

A tap on the bedroom door made her jump. "Who is it?" she asked, staring at the door, which had no lock, and praying it wouldn't open on her. And then she realized what an inane question she'd just asked and rolled her eyes.

"It's Luke. Breakfast will be ready in fifteen minutes, if you're hungry. And, um, if you need something to wear, you can snag a pair of sweats and a T-shirt out of my bottom drawer."

"What makes you think I don't have anything to wear?"

"You going to tell me you do?" he asked her. Or was he daring her?

"I'll be a half hour," she said, choosing to ignore his challenge. No human being could possibly get ready for anything in fifteen minutes.

Baxter tugged on her skirt. "Mom, can't I go down now? I'm starved. And I already washed up."

She glanced at her son, saw that he had indeed washed his face and tugged a comb through his hair. He was wearing the same clothes as yesterday, but that couldn't be helped. Still, she didn't want to let him out of her sight.

"Jasmine?" Luke's voice came through the door, deep and soft. "You're five hundred miles from whatever happened in Illinois. I'll watch him close, I promise. Why don't you let him come on down to breakfast?"

She glared at the door, almost let the words on the tip of her tongue spill out, but bit them back at the last possible moment. She swallowed hard, ignoring the redneck and turning to her son. "Bax, I'll hurry as fast as I can, okay, baby?" she said softly. "But please, don't go down to breakfast without me."

He pouted, sighed, hung his head. "Okay, Mom. I'll wait for you." Then he turned to the closed door. "We'll be down in a few minutes, Mr. Brand."

There was a hesitation. "Okay, Baxter. I'll keep it warm for you."

Jasmine hugged him close. "Thank you, hon." Then she glanced at the clock on the bedside stand and wondered if she could break the land speed record for shower, hair and makeup. She yanked open the bottom dresser drawer, and fished out a pair of gray sweatpants and a white T-shirt with some logo or other on the front. She didn't bother to look too closely, because it didn't really matter what the design was, it was still going to look like she was wearing a tent. She kissed Bax on the cheek and headed into the adjoining bathroom. "I'm gonna leave the door open a tiny bit, baby," she told Baxter. "So all you need to do is call me if you need me, okay?"

"Okay," he said, climbing onto the bed with a remote in his hand. He aimed it at the TV set, and she knew he would be okay for a few minutes.

* * *

Luke thought it odder than odd that the woman wouldn't let the kid out of her sight long enough to have breakfast when he was obviously hungry. What kind of a mother was she, anyway? Even his own overprotective, clinging mother hadn't been *that* bad. Hell, it didn't sit right with him. And he tried to wait, he really did, but fifteen minutes came and went, and he still didn't hear that boy coming down the stairs.

Fine. If she didn't want her son down here alone with the big bad Brand, he would just take matters into his own hands. He lifted the stoneware plate from the spot he'd set for Baxter at the table, heaped it full of food, filled a glass with milk and headed up the stairs. Once again he tapped on his own bedroom door, trying not to slop the milk as he did it.

"Who is it?" the little guy asked.

The sound of his voice brought a smile to Luke's face for some reason. Hell, the kid was cute. "It's Luke. I figured there was no sense making you wait for breakfast, so I brought you up a plateful, if that's okay."

The door whipped open so fast Luke almost dropped the plate. "You bet it's okay. Thanks, Mr. Brand."

Luke smiled, holding out the plate to the kid, looking nervously past him. Baxter grabbed his arm and tugged him right inside, though. He could hear the shower running, and the bathroom door was only half-closed. The woman wasn't shy, that was for sure. Then again, she probably hadn't expected him to come back. Much less come all the way inside this time. "Come on," Baxter said. "I'm watching *Star Rangers!*"

Luke glanced at the TV set, at the super heroes spin-kicking their way across the screen and the bad guys. "That's my little cousin Bubba's favorite show, too."

Baxter tugged Luke to the bed, and Luke sat down. The little guy did, too, but on the nearby chair, and he dug right into his food. In between bites, he said, "There are kids here?"

"Oh, a couple. Bubba's the closest to your age. You might get to meet him later on."

Baxter smiled, pushed his glasses up on his nose and kept on eating. "I knew there was bacon," he said. "At home, every Sunday morning, my mom gets up early, and she makes this big breakfast for all of us, with bacon."

"Oh yeah? For all of you?" Luke asked, sensing a shot at some information. And more than that. He hadn't exactly pegged Jasmine as a Sunday breakfast kind of a mother.

"Me and Aunt Rosebud and Mom," he explained.

"The three of you live together, then?"

The boy's face fell. He stopped eating, stared at

the floor. "We used to. But…not anymore. Aunt Rosebud's gone to live with the angels now."

Luke felt like a rat. His prying had ruined the kid's breakfast. What kind of a bully was he, anyway? "Hey, I have some friends up there, too," he said, forcing a smile. "I'll bet your Aunt Rosebud and my buddy Buck are having a heck of a good time with those angels."

Baxter lifted his head a little. "You think so?"

"Well, sure I do. Buck, he loved a good Sunday breakfast himself."

"And did he like to dance, too? Aunt Rosebud's a great dancer. Almost as good as my mom."

So his mother danced? Interesting. "He loved to dance, Baxter. Why, I'll bet they're gonna be best friends before long."

"Yeah," Baxter said. He smiled a little, and even started to pick at the food again. "Yeah, they will for sure." Then he paused and looked up. "Your friend Buck, he wasn't a bad guy, was he?"

"No, Bax. He was one of the best good guys I ever knew."

Baxter smiled more fully and devoted his attention to his food. Luke wanted to ask him about those bad guys he kept referring to, but he thought that just then it was more important for the child to eat than for Luke to have his curiosity satisfied. He could wait for his answers.

It occurred to him then that the shower had stopped running. And he turned to glance toward the bathroom door just as the woman stepped through it, wearing nothing but a towel and an expression of surprise.

"What are you doing in here?" she blurted.

"I'm sorry." *Look away,* he told his eyes. They wouldn't budge. He couldn't make them budge. She was a totally different woman now. An incredibly beautiful woman. "B-Baxter was hungry and I, um, I felt bad making him wait, so I brought his breakfast up."

"And stayed to supervise while he ate it?"

He couldn't get over the difference in her with her face scrubbed so clean it glowed pink, and her hair wet and plastered to her head. He'd missed everything about her besides the thick coat of makeup. She had the face of a wood fairy. Tiny, elfin nose and a small, rounded chin. Sculpted cheekbones and full lips. And those eyes. Why on earth had she ever thought she needed to plaster coats of color over those eyes? They were huge and round and dark brown in color. He suddenly wished she would smile. He needed, suddenly, to see that face with a smile.

She didn't, but he kept looking anyway. His gaze skimmed down her neck and over her shoulders and arms. Toned. Firm. The woman was as fit as any he'd seen. She looked as if she worked out with weights or something. The towel hung loosely to the upper half of her thighs, and they, too, were shapely and toned. Her bare feet...she had the cutest little feet....

"You finished?" she asked.

He snapped his gaze up to her eyes and felt the skin under his collar get hot. "I, um...yeah. Yeah, I am." Unable to say anything remotely intelligent, he turned to leave. "Your breakfast is still warm, you know, if you want it. Although, maybe you don't. I didn't think...you probably don't eat that kind of..." As he spoke, he glanced over his shoulder and saw her munching a slice of bacon she'd snitched from her son's plate. "Or...maybe you do." He shrugged, more baffled than before, and opened the door to leave.

"Luke," she said.

He turned.

"That was nice, what you did. Bringing Baxter's breakfast up like that. Thank you."

He felt a smile tug at one side of his mouth. "That's okay."

"I really will only be a few more minutes," she said. And amazingly, incredibly, she smiled. Just a little bit. It was halfhearted, just a slight pulling of her lips upward at the corners. But even then it transformed her face. Made her eyes sparkle and dug dimples into her cheeks.

Oh, hell.

"Well, good. I'll be downstairs, then." Finally he got out of there, closing the door behind him and realizing he hadn't really been breathing in several minutes. Or it felt like it, anyway. He let the air out of him in a rush and headed for the kitchen. What was the matter with him, anyway? She doled out a grudging halfhearted thanks with an eyedropper, and he was reacting as if she'd kissed his feet in gratitude.

The man must be some kind of Neanderthal. It was obvious, because he didn't own a hair dryer. And his shampoo had been that practical kind with the conditioner already mixed in. He was definitely primitive. And big. His sweatpants and shirt positively hung on her.

But he'd been kind to Baxter, and that meant something. Even though she knew perfectly well it was more than likely all for show. An act to get what he wanted, win her trust and then stab her in the back, or get her into his bed and then stab her in the back, or whatever. They always wanted something.

Still, at least he made an effort to appear to be…kind of sweet. Maybe even a little shy. The way he'd stuttered and stammered when she'd walked out of the bathroom in a towel. It was far from the wolf whistles she'd come to expect from men when they saw her in various states of undress.

He'd seemed dumbstuck. Stood there with his soft brown hair and his baby-blue eyes and just stared at her.

So he was at least making an effort. It was a good job, too. She almost believed it was real.

She tugged a brush through her hair, wincing with every pull. And the whole time, her stomach was growling at the smell of the food Baxter was wolfing down in the bedroom.

Lifting her gaze to the bathroom mirror, she gave up on the hair, pulling it back into a ponytail. She did not have hair that was conducive to ponytails, she decided, as strand after curling strand escaped the confines of the pink hair tie she'd found in her purse.

Okay, fine. There was no hope for the hair, but at least she could do something about her face. She picked up Rosebud's big bag. She'd already taken her own smaller purse from inside it. Now she dumped the rest of the contents out onto the big countertop beside the bathroom sink…and stopped dead as the black revolver clunked heavily onto the tiny blue ceramic tiles.

Her throat went dry. She glanced toward the bedroom. Baxter was still engrossed in the TV program and the meal, so she pushed the door closed just a little more and carefully picked up the handgun. She wasn't familiar with guns or the way they worked, so it took her a moment to find the catch that released the round cylinder, allowing it to flip outward. There were bullets in each of the six small holes.

"Loaded," she whispered. "Damn you, Rosebud, how could you have kept a loaded gun so close to my baby?'' She quickly pulled the bullets out, one by one, holding the bunch of them in her palm. She didn't like guns. She was against them, thought they should be banned, for heaven's sake. But she wasn't about to give this one up. Not while Leo and his sleazy murdering friend, the dirty cop, might still be hunting her. Maybe if it were her alone they wanted—but it wasn't. They wanted Baxter. And she would fight to the death and burn every last principle she had for her little boy. Still, she would have to be very careful with this.

She found a small bottle of pain reliever among the articles that had spilled out of the bag and snatched it up, pouring the tablets into the toilet. Then she put the bullets into the bottle and capped it. Childproof cover. Good. She zipped the bottle into a small compartment in the big bag. Then she put the revolver into her own smaller purse.

"Mommy, can't we go downstairs yet?"

She glanced at the makeup scattered all over the counter and sighed in defeat. It just wasn't going to happen this morning. And it didn't matter, anyway. Hell, no one would recognize her looking the way she looked today. Like some fresh-faced farm girl in desperate need of her first trip to the salon. Maybe it was for the best. Holding Rosebud's bag at the edge, she scooped everything back into it and hung it on a peg in the wall. "I'm coming, baby."

She took her son's hand and led him out into the

hallway, then down the stairs. It was a nice house. It was a crying shame Rosebud hadn't lived to inherit it the way her mother had obviously intended. She would have loved it here. The staircase was old, too steep and too narrow, but the banister was heavy gleaming hardwood that had to be worth a fortune. She ran her hand over it slowly all the way to the bottom.

"It's all one piece," Luke Brand said.

Jasmine looked up, not expecting to see him standing just beyond the bottom step, staring up at her. "What?"

"The banister. It's cut from one continuous piece of hard maple, all the way up and along the landing."

"Oh."

He shrugged, shifted his feet. "It seemed really important to the assessors when they were out here last month. I guess they don't make them like that anymore. Just thought you'd be interested."

"It's…interesting all right."

"Well, anyway. Food's out here." Turning, he walked beneath the wide brick archway into the dining room. It was different now, with the morning sun slanting through the place. The big French doors on the far side of the room looked like a giant wall painting of lush green meadows that rolled endlessly. For a moment she just blinked at it.

"The…uh…drapes were closed last night, so

you maybe didn't notice the doors then. I put them in myself.''

Turning, she looked at him with brows raised. ''Did you?''

''It was just a back wall. Dark as a dungeon in here.'' He pulled out her chair. ''And I figured the place was as good as my own, so I didn't mind investing a little time and money in it.''

She looked at him, standing there, behind her chair. No one had ever pulled a chair out for her in her life that she could recall. She sat down and glimpsed the French doors again. Brass handled and hinged, the trim around them fit perfectly even at the corners. He'd done a good job. And there was a small, octagon-shaped deck beyond them. She would bet that hadn't been part of the original house, either.

Luke Brand was fetching plates from the oven now, setting one in front of her, heaped with enough food for three women, at least. Then he sat down across from her with his own.

''You didn't need to wait for me.''

He shrugged. ''I eat alone all the time. Decided company for breakfast might be nice for a change.''

She pressed her lips together, then turned to catch sight of Baxter. He was wandering the house, pausing at every window to look outside. He wanted to go out. She knew he did. It was killing her to keep him so cooped up.

''He can go outside and play, you know. The

road's a hundred feet from the house, and even if it weren't, there's no such thing as traffic out here.''

She averted her eyes. ''I'll take him out later on.''

''Don't let him out of your sight much, do you?''

She looked at him quickly. ''You have an opinion on my parenting skills, Mr. Brand?''

He shrugged. ''Guess you'd know more about that than I would. I've never had a kid. Don't know much about 'em. Except that they need room to grow.''

She shook her head. ''You're right, you don't know much about kids.''

He nodded at her plate. ''You're not eating.''

She shoveled a bite into her mouth without looking first. It turned out to be a portion of omelette that just about melted in her mouth. It was all she could do to keep from closing her eyes in ecstasy. And though she tried to keep her expression static, he saw right through it and smiled that charming smile of his. ''Good, isn't it?''

She nodded, swallowing, and reached for the coffee. It was as heavenly as the omelette had been. ''You're a chef or something, aren't you?''

''No. I'm a trucker. Or…was. I sold my rig to buy this place.''

She lifted her brows, surprised by his answer. So he'd given up his livelihood to be here—and then she'd come along to claim the place. No wonder he'd been less than friendly last night. At least, until he'd met Baxter. "What are you going to do for a living now?"

He shrugged. "I've got time to figure it out. There seem to be enough odd jobs in town to keep me in demand until I decide."

"Odd jobs?"

He nodded. "Yeah, mostly courtesy of my cousins. Let's see, between them they have a cattle ranch, a horse ranch, a dude ranch, a veterinary clinic, a martial arts school—"

She held up a hand. "I get it. You've got a lot of family in town."

"You didn't even let me get to the P.I., the sheriff, the archaeologist and the shrink."

She tried to keep her face expressionless when he mentioned the sheriff. But she couldn't help but flash back to that cop, Petronella, standing over Rosebud's body, looking up at her. The same man she'd seen commit a murder—the man who'd taken a shot at her son.

"Actually, now that I think about it, you could probably find work with any of them, if you're looking."

She shook herself out of the disturbing memory and glanced into the next room to see that Baxter had settled down in front of the TV again. It wasn't good for him, all that television. "I would think you'd be pushing me to leave here, not giving me job tips that might keep me around even longer."

He shrugged. "This thing with the property will

get settled one way or another no matter what I
do,'' he said. ''Frankly, I'm more concerned about
your son right now than I am about who wins a
fight over a house.''

She tipped her head to one side. He was trying
to get to her by feigning concern for Baxter. It was
low. She'd seen it before. Never done quite this
well or convincingly, though.

''So what do you do for a living, Jasmine?''

She looked him dead in the eye. ''I'm a dancer.''

His brows rose. ''Really? What, ballet?''

Still watching him, she said, ''Exotic.''

His face stilled, mouth frozen into a thin line as
he slowly digested that bit of information. ''You're
a—'' Glancing toward Baxter, he lowered his voice
to a whisper. ''You're a stripper?''

''That's right. So about that job you're going to
help me find…''

''Mommy, Mommy, look! Horses! Real live
horses! Just like on TV!''

Jasmine had to pull hard to yank her gaze away
from Luke Brand's probing one, but she did, getting
to her feet and going to the living room just as
Baxter pulled the door open and ran outside.

There were people out there. Strangers on horse-
back, riding up to the house like something out of
an old western. Jasmine sprinted after her son, her
heart in her throat, and caught him just as he
reached the dangerous hooves. She scooped him up,

held him hard, her heart pounding as she turned and carried him back toward the house.

Luke stood there on the top step, looking at her, a deep frown etched between his brows. Then he looked past her, and his expression changed. He smiled, waved. "Garrett, Chelsea, good to see you. Hey, Bubba! How's my best cowboy?"

"I rode all the way all by myself," a child's voice shouted.

Jasmine lifted her head, turning slowly to look more closely at the strangers from whom she'd just rescued her son. The man was so big he would have been frightening, except for the warm, easy smile he wore. He touched the brim of his hat and gave her a nod before dismounting and reaching up to help the woman down.

She was an attractive woman, probably in her thirties, with brown hair in a long ponytail. She put her hands on the man's shoulders as he helped her down. Then they both turned to look at the little boy, with his dark hair and striking blue eyes, sitting atop a pony, wearing a cowboy hat that was too big for him.

"These are some of my cousins, Garrett and Chelsea Brand, and their son, Bubba," Luke said to Jasmine. "Folks, this is Jasmine, and her son, Baxter."

Baxter had locked eyes on the little boy, riding that pony all by himself, and Jasmine knew she would never hear the end of this one. Even as she looked on, the boy called Bubba swung one leg over his saddle and leaped to the ground. It was all Jasmine could do not to shout a warning, certain he would hurt himself. But he didn't. He marched right up to Baxter instead.

"Hi."

"Hi," Baxter said, pushing his glasses up on his nose.

"You want to pet my pony?"

"Could I?"

"I don't think…" Jasmine began.

The woman spoke then. "The pony's gentle as a kitten," she said. "I wouldn't let Bubba anywhere near it if it were dangerous at all."

Bubba looked sturdy and strong compared to Baxter, though, Jasmine thought. He must be at least a couple of years older. And what might not be dangerous at all to him might very well be a threat to her own delicate little boy.

"Please, Mom?" Baxter asked.

"Oh, all right. But no riding on that thing."

"Okay!" Baxter and Bubba headed over to the pony. Meanwhile Garrett was tying the other two horses up to a rail that seemed to have been made for that very purpose.

"Shall we go inside to talk?" Garrett asked.

Talk…about what? Jasmine wondered.

"Oh, let's sit on the porch, so we can keep an eye on the boys, hmm?" Chelsea said with a glance at Jasmine.

"You probably think I'm an overprotective lunatic."

Chelsea shook her head. "Why should I think that? Luke says you're from Chicago. I'm from New York. I know full well that, in cities like those, letting your child out of your sight is practically courting disaster."

Oddly enough, it seemed the woman understood.

"It's different out here, but it takes time for a mom to get comfortable with that. So it's perfectly natural for you to want to keep a close watch on little Baxter. Heck, I'd be worried if you didn't!"

She *seemed* very kind...and genuine. That didn't mean she was. In Jasmine's experience, most people were not what they seemed. Still, she walked up onto the porch and sat in one of the white wicker chairs. Luke took the other one, while Chelsea and Garrett settled into the matching love seat. "So, um, I guess Luke has already told you about me."

"I called them this morning," Luke explained. "I thought they could help us get this mess straightened out."

She lifted her brows. "I don't understand how."

"Well, for one thing," Garrett said, "I knew your mother."

Jasmine's throat went dry as she stared at him. For just an instant she thought of her own drunken tramp of a mother who'd died young and left Jasmine on her own at fifteen. But then she realized these people all thought she was Rosebud. Jenny

Lee Walker. So the mother he was referring to was Rosebud's mother—the woman who'd left her this house.

"Oh," she said finally. "How well did you know her?"

"Almost as well as I knew my own," Garrett said with a friendly smile, leaning back in his chair.

Jasmine braced herself. This was not a good sign.

Chapter 6

Luke saw Jasmine's reaction to Garrett's revelation that he'd known her mother. Fear. It was plain and easily read, even though she covered it fast. There had been a slight widening of those already huge dark eyes and the tiniest flare of her nostrils. Why?

"It was before you were born, of course," Garrett said, comfortable in the chair, one arm slung casually around his wife's shoulders. "Helena's husband had died young, left her widowed and alone, with this big house to care for and two hundred acres to farm. Of course, that's not a lot of land by Texas standards, but it's a lot to expect one woman to handle alone. She was lonely, I think."

"Well, sure she was," Chelsea put in. "Gosh, what did she do to make ends meet?"

"I was getting to that." Garrett smiled indulgently at his wife, tapped her nose with his forefinger.

The woman was way too relaxed, Jasmine thought vaguely. She sat there all calm and content watching the boys pet the pony, while Jasmine was nearly jumping out of her seat every time the beast moved. And the conversation had her nearly as jittery as the big hooves did.

"Helena needed some income to help keep the wolves at bay. Meanwhile, my own mother was struggling through with five young'uns and no help other than a husband who was raised to believe caring for the kids was women's work." He shrugged. "So it was a match made in heaven. Helena came by almost every day and helped out around the house, for, oh, about a year. Then all of the sudden she up and moved away."

"But she didn't sell the place," Luke said. "I wonder why?"

"She might have considered it the last part of her husband she had to cling to," Chelsea said. "Or maybe she intended to keep it for her daughter."

"Well, that's what she did," Jasmine said softly.

Garrett took a breath and sighed. "Luke, you've looked over this packet of paperwork Jasmine brought along?"

Luke nodded.

"And does it look to you like her claim is legit?"

Luke faced her squarely. She imagined he would

try to bluff his way through, make her out to be a fraud and then have his cousin the sheriff boot her out of here. Instead he said, "Yeah. It looks perfectly legit." He sighed then. "But that isn't gonna stop this place from being auctioned for back taxes next week—unless she can come up with fifty grand by then."

"Fifty..." She blinked her eyes in shock at the sheer size of the debt. Then she shook herself and sat up straighter. "Next week is next week. Right now, today, I am the rightful owner of this place, and I have every right to stay here."

Luke nodded slowly. "That's all well and good. But I've paid my rent to the lawyer your mother left in charge of things for the full month, in advance, and I have every right to stay here, too."

"Maybe you should go see the lawyer and let him decide," Chelsea suggested, her tone gentling, as if she were negotiating a truce between two squabbling children.

"That's a good start, but it won't happen until Monday. Buzz Montana's out of town for the weekend. Some case up north. And no judge is going to be willing to hear this on short notice without all the information in front of him. So even if you two decide to fight this out in court, you'd have to wait at least that long," Garrett said.

"I'm not leaving," Jasmine said.

"I'm not budging, either," Luke replied, crossing his arms over his chest. "Possession is nine-tenths of the law, isn't that right, Garrett? I mean, if I move out now, I might lose whatever meager claim I do have to this place.'' Garrett nodded, and Luke went on. ''Look, I'm not trying to be a hard case here, Jasmine. And the last thing I want is to see you and Baxter without a place to stay. But this place—it means more to me than you can know. I gave up my life's work for this—I can't just hand it over without a word.''

Jasmine frowned at him. God, he was good. He almost had her feeling sorry for him.

Chelsea got to her feet. ''Look, forgive me for being dense here, but I really fail to see the problem.''

All three of them looked at her as if she were insane.

She just waved a hand toward the house. ''Will you look at the size of this place? You telling me there's not room here for one man, one woman and a tiny little fella like Baxter over there? For one lousy weekend? Come on, people, this one's a no-brainer.''

Pursing his lips, rubbing his chin, Garrett nodded slowly. ''She does have a point.''

''Aw, come on, Garrett,'' Luke all but moaned.

Garrett lifted his eyebrows. Then, slowly, he got to his feet. ''Take a walk with me, cousin?''

Luke frowned but didn't argue. Garrett headed down the steps. Luke went with him.

Chelsea smiled at Jasmine. "Don't you worry. Garrett will set him straight."

"Will he?"

"Sure. Now let's talk about the clothing situation here. I'm assuming what you're wearing is not a fashion choice."

Jasmine glanced down at the way-too-big sweats and T-shirt. "They're not even mine."

"No, I didn't really think you'd have chosen that particular T-shirt."

She glanced down at her own chest, saw the bulldog logo, groaned. "I pulled it on so fast I didn't even look to see what was on it."

"The back's worse," Chelsea said. "Built Like A Mack Truck, it says."

Jasmine met Chelsea's eyes, saw the humor in them and heard herself laugh. She couldn't believe the sound was coming from her, not with all that had happened in the past few days. But somehow the woman had put her at ease and managed to make her laugh. Her smile lingered, and she said, "Wait a minute, I think I've figured it out. You must be the shrink in the family. Luke mentioned there was one."

Chelsea smiled. "Guilty, I guess. I'm a psychologist. I mostly work with woman who've been victims of domestic violence."

"Hell, you must have no shortage of patients, then."

"Unfortunately, there always seem to be plenty.

Even out here.'' She sighed, rather sadly. ''But
that's off the subject, isn't it?''

Jasmine shrugged, turning her attention toward
her son again. ''I forgot what the subject was.''

''Your clothes. Or lack thereof. Seems like you
left Chicago in a bit of a hurry.''

Jasmine sent her a sideways glance.

''Not that I'm prying. I'm not. I mean...unless
you *want* to talk about it.''

''I don't.''

''Okay. At any rate, Luke mentioned the situation this morning.'' She got up as she spoke,
stepped off the porch to her horse and tugged open
a leather pouch strapped to the back of the saddle.
She pulled a bag out of it and brought it back up
the steps with her. ''I brought a few things for you.
Just to tide you two over until you have a chance
to do some shopping.''

Jasmine was so stunned she couldn't even speak.
She pressed her fingertips to the front of her throat,
where it felt like the air had frozen.

''It's no big deal,'' Chelsea assured her. ''A couple pairs of Bubba's jeans—hell, he grows out of
them so fast I can barely keep up, anyway. A few
shirts, and a handful of my stuff for you...although
looking at you, I think you'll swim in my clothes.''

''Even if that were true, it wouldn't be for long.
With Luke cooking the way he does, and me not
having time to work out for three days running
now...''

"You should come with me to the dojo this afternoon!" Chelsea said, as if it were the most exciting idea in history.

Jasmine lifted her brows. "The dojo?"

"The kids take karate lessons. Grown-ups, too, from time to time. Garrett's brother Ben owns the place. He'd be glad to let us use part of the gym. And then you can tell me how you stay looking like you do."

Jasmine lowered her head. Was it possible this woman really was as nice as she seemed to be? Just like Luke, she was either genuine, or a hell of an actress. "I guess I could. But I'm not sure about letting Bax do anything as violent as karate."

"It's not violent, Jasmine. Not when it's taught in keeping with its true principles. It's spiritual. Reserve judgment and see for yourself, okay?"

"Okay."

"Good."

Jasmine glanced over at Bax, saw him watching longingly as Bubba climbed up into the saddle and rode his pony in a small circle, demonstrating some technique, she supposed. A twinge of mother guilt tugged at her heart, but she held her ground. Baxter wasn't like this robust little Bubba. He was frail, delicate. He tended to bruise very easily.

"How old is he?" Chelsea asked, following her gaze.

"Seven. Just seven." Jasmine looked at the bigger, sturdier boy and asked, "How about Bubba?"

"His name is actually Ethan, you know. I fought the nickname from day one, but you just can't win against a town full of macho cowboy uncles. He's almost six."

Jasmine blinked. "Six? But he's so big!" She shook her head in disbelief. She would have pegged the child as at least eight or nine. "He must take after Garrett in size," she mused aloud. There must be some reason why he seemed so much bigger and more solid than her own precious son.

Chelsea said, "He's adopted, so that can't be it. I tend to think it's just all this fresh air and sunshine. Quinn's the best place in the world to raise children." She smiled warmly. "Your Baxter is just gonna love it here."

"We aren't gonna be here that long," Jasmine said, and then she wished she could take the words back, because she saw Chelsea's puzzled reaction. If this house were truly her inheritance, why wouldn't she be planning to live in it?

It probably sounded suspect to this woman. But then again, it was really none of her business.

Luke leaned against an elm tree in the backyard, where he had a clear view of the kids out front messing with the pony. "Look at the poor, scrawny little fella," he said. "He wants to ride Bubba's pony so bad he can hardly stand it, but his anal, overprotective mother is too afraid he'll get a bruise or a scratch to let him."

He turned his gaze to Garrett. "So what did you want to talk to me about?"

"Uh, that."

"What?"

"What you just said. About Jasmine."

Luke shook his head slowly. "She's a nut."

"She's a woman, and she's on her own with that boy, and she's running scared," Garrett said, hunkering down and resting his elbows across his knees.

Luke lifted his brows. "You got that feeling, too, huh?"

"It's pretty obvious she's in some kind of trouble."

"Yeah." He drew a breath, not liking the tight, anxious feeling in his chest.

"Now, I know you haven't been a part of the family for all that long, but I thought you'd picked up on enough to know better than to act the way you are toward a woman in trouble, Luke."

Luke frowned. "What do you mean? I let her spend the night. I gave her my own bed. And I made her breakfast, for crying out loud."

"And this morning you're ready to boot her out."

"She's trying to take my house away from me!"

"Maybe she's got a legitimate claim," Garrett said, his tone deep and calm. "But that's not why you want her out, and I think you know it."

Luke sighed, averted his eyes, then peeked down

at Garrett again. "I don't think spending the week-end under the same roof with her is the smartest thing for me to do, is all."

"Why not?" Garrett asked.

"*Why not?* Hell, Garrett, have you taken a good look at that woman?"

Garrett pursed his lips. "So, you kind of like her."

"No. I don't. I don't like her at all. And I don't want to. She's not the kind of woman I want to get involved with, not in any way, shape or form. Be-sides, she's lying. I can tell."

"How?"

"She won't show me any ID, Garrett. We don't even know she *is* Jenny Lee Walker."

Garrett sighed. "Well, now, it wouldn't be too bright to come all the way out here and try to claim the place if she couldn't prove she was who she says she is, would it, Luke? Why would she lie about something that's so simple to check out?"

Luke lifted his brows. "Simple to check out?"

"Sure. We just check with the Illinois DMV, trace her plate number, get a copy of her driver's license down here and take a gander at the photo. What could be easier?"

Pursing his lips, Luke said, "Do it."

"Do it?"

"Please? I've got a feeling about her, Garrett. She's trouble with a capital *T*. Run the plates, too, while you're at it."

Garrett shrugged. "Fine, I'll do it. Have to wait till Monday, though. The DMV won't be open on the weekend. Come Monday, I'll put in a call and they'll fax me the photo. Okay?"

He sighed. "Okay."

"Meanwhile, you need to straighten up and be a Brand. You got a woman and a kid in trouble, with nowhere to go. You keep her here. Put her up until we settle this thing. And try being nice to her."

"Is that an order?"

Garrett smiled. "Considering I'm the closest thing to a big brother you got, cousin, yep, consider it an order. But, uh...be careful."

Luke straightened away from the tree. "Careful? Why? Do you think she's dangerous?"

"Hoo-yeah," Garrett said. "But not the way you think. See, there's this genetic defect that seems to run through the males in the Brand clan. Women who are trouble with a capital *T*—we tend to fall head over heels for 'em."

"What, are you kidding me?"

"Nope." He shook his head. "And seeing as how you're scared to death to be left alone with her—even while swearing up and down she's not the kind of woman you want to be involved with—well, that tells me one thing, cuz."

"Oh yeah? What?"

Garrett got upright, adjusted his hat. "You're probably already doomed." He slapped Luke on the shoulder with a sympathetic shake of his head and started back around to the house.

"What the hell is that supposed to mean? Garrett!"

But his big cousin was already vanishing from sight.

"I need to go into town for a few things. Do you want to ride along?"

She sensed the man was trying to make conversation, trying to be polite. But she also knew he wasn't doing it because he wanted to. His cousin must have told him to be nice to her. After he'd come back from his chat with the big guy, he'd told her she could stay here with him "until things were settled." Which, she assumed, meant until he could boot her out with the law firmly behind him.

At least he hadn't tried to get her into bed yet. Which was somehow both reassuring and insulting at the same time. Maybe he didn't like women.

Or maybe he just didn't like *her*.

"I want to, Mom!" Baxter said. "Can't we, please?"

She frowned, not wanting her son out in public—but then again, she reasoned, no one had shown up at the door with a gun yet. And if Leo or Petronella or any of their goons had been able to figure out where she'd gone, they would have. She had no doubt of that. So that probably meant she and Baxter were safe here. For the moment, at least.

"Please, Mom?"

She shrugged. "I do need to pick up a few things. All right, I guess so."

She glanced down at her attire. She'd put on a pair of the jeans Chelsea Brand had brought over and a white cotton button-down shirt. Her hair was still in a ponytail, her feet in her open-toed spiky-heeled boots and her face downright naked of makeup. "I'd better see what I can do about the way I look first."

"You're right," Luke said.

She looked up fast, ready to shoot back. "What?"

"You need some decent walking shoes, or sneakers, or something," he said. "Course, I can't help with that, being that everything I have is a hefty size eleven. But I *do* have a good rugged set of fingernail clippers if you want to use them."

She swung her gaze to his, her jaw gaping. "What the hell is that supposed to mean?" Holding up a hand, palm out, she studied her nails. They were gorgeous. Long and curving and airbrushed. "What's wrong with my nails?"

"Well, nothing—if you're a cougar. What are you plannin' to do with those things, shred cabbage?" He sent Baxter a grin and a wink, and Baxter laughed out loud, holding his belly.

"I suppose you could carve your initials in the elm tree out back, if you wanted," Luke went on.

"Or maybe in your forehead," she countered.

But it was tough to hold on to her anger when her son was laughing so hard. His little cheeks were turning red now, and his glasses had slid down his nose. "Oh, so you think it's funny, do you?" she said to her son. "I thought you liked my nails?"

He grinned so hard his dimples had dimples. "I think they're pretty, Mom." Giggle, chortle, chuckle. "Really."

"Yeah, sure you do." She scowled at him. "So am I allowed to go put on some makeup, or is that going to start another laugh riot down here?"

"You're pretty enough without it, Mom," Baxter said. "Isn't she, Luke?"

Luke looked like the kid had just kicked him in the belly. He stuttered, he stammered, he got red faced. "Well...I...er...um...just...uh..."

"I'll be down in ten minutes," she said, not even waiting for his verdict on her prettiness, or lack thereof. "You guys wait, or else."

"Okay," Baxter called, smiling all over. "But don't put on too much, okay, Mom?"

Luke was still stammering.

She met her time limit with two minutes to spare, heading back downstairs with her hair now loose and thoroughly brushed, and wearing minimal makeup—just enough to make her feel human.

"Okay, I'm ready," she said.

Luke was fidgeting near the doorway. He'd been looking outside at something and only turned to face her when she spoke. Then he offered a crooked smile. "You really do look just fine without all the goop on your face," he said.

Jasmine frowned. "Was that supposed to be an apology or a compliment?"

He shrugged, turning his attention back outside. She followed his gaze to see Baxter running through the tall summer grasses and wildflowers outside. "I figured it would be okay as long as I kept an eye on him," Luke said.

She lifted her brows. "He has allergies. He'll probably be up all night coughing. I'll have to pick up some antihistamine while we're out."

Luke started to say something nasty. She could tell by the look on his face and the quick beginning of a word that broke off so fast it came out sounding like a primal grunt. He bit his lip, drew a breath.

"What?" she asked, almost challenged.

"Nothing. I, um...I was going to say if you're short on cash, I could loan you enough to get you by for a while."

She blinked in surprise, then shook her head. "That cousin of yours really does have some influence with you, doesn't he?"

"Why do you say so?"

She shrugged. "Because I know perfectly well you'd sooner see me tarred and feathered and branded with a scarlet *S* for Stripper than holed up here in your precious house with you for a few days. And yet here you are, chivalrously offering me a loan."

He narrowed his eyes on her. "Look, I was just trying to be nice."

"Try being honest, instead. It's so much more satisfying."

"Oh yeah?"

"Yeah."

"Fine. I'll be honest. I think you're lying through your teeth about who you are, and I think you're running like hell from something or someone, and you're scared half out of your wits. And so's that boy out there. And maybe that's why you're hovering over the poor kid so close you're damn near smothering him, but I don't think so. From the looks of him, you've been doing that for a long time now. So maybe whatever happened to send you running out of Chicago has only turned it up a notch or two. But either way, the kid's the one suffering for it, and you need to ease up on him."

She glared at him. "You dare to criticize my parenting skills!"

"That's right. I do."

"What do you know?" she all but shouted. "You've never been a parent!"

"No, but I've been a kid!"

"To hell with you. You don't know anything. That boy out there is my entire life. He's everything to me. Do you have any idea what it's like to love something that much? So much that if you lost it you'd just stop being? You'd just curl up and dry up and vanish? Do you have any idea how scary that is? I'd do anything for my son. And I have!''

He went quiet for a moment, staring at her as the high color in his face eased down a notch. Then he said, ''Like...the dancing?''

She lowered her eyes. ''I'm not ashamed of what I do. Dancing is art. The female body is beautiful. Women have been performing erotic dance for over five thousand years.''

He raised his eyebrows. ''But not for drunken perverts, for the most part.''

''Thanks. Jerk.''

He shrugged. ''I meant...it can't be fun.''

''Don't knock it till you've tried it.'' She was being sarcastic, but she didn't expect him to pick up on that.

''Come on, gimme a break, will you? I meant, it's a hell of a sacrifice to do what you do for a living. You must love him a lot.''

''I thought we'd already established that.''

He sighed, rolled his eyes. ''You ready to go, or what?''

She sent him a scowl and pushed past him out the door. Her feet tapped across the wood floor of the front porch, and she glanced out toward where Baxter had been playing.

He wasn't there.

''Bax?'' She tapped down the steps. ''Hon, where are you?''

''Up here, Mom! Look at me!''

She followed his voice and spotted him as the screen door banged closed and Luke stepped up beside her. Baxter was hanging upside down from a tree limb about fifteen feet in the air. To her, it looked more like a thousand feet, but her logical mind said fifteen. Even so, her blood ran icy cold. "Don't move!" she cried. "Don't you move, Baxter!" She ran down the steps and out toward the tree with Luke on her heels.

He said, "Will you stop panicking? You're scaring him."

"*I'm* scaring *him?*" She got to the tree trunk. Her shoes were long gone. She'd kicked them off on the way, and now she grabbed a low limb and pulled herself easily up onto it.

"Hey, wait a minute! What do you think you're— *Jasmine!*"

She wished he would shut up. "Stay still, Baxter," she called. "Mama's coming, baby. Just don't move."

She monkey-climbed her way up higher and higher. Her son was talking calmly, carrying on what sounded for all the world like a normal conversation with Luke, while she climbed like a wild woman. Finally, finally, she reached the limb where Baxter had been hanging. Only he wasn't there.

Her heart hammered so hard she thought it was coming through her chest, and she shot a glance toward the ground, half expecting to see his broken body lying there. Instead, she heard laughter and

saw her son being held in the big arms of Luke
Brand. Luke was grinning like a loon and ruffling
Baxter's hair, and Bax was laughing out loud up at
him.

Luke looked up. "Hey, he's okay. You can come
down now."

She blew her hair out of her face. "How did you
get down there so fast, Baxter?"

He smiled. "I just jumped. Luke catched me."

"You jumped?" She glared at Luke. "He
jumped?"

"Well, don't look at me, it wasn't my idea." He
set Bax on his feet, brushed the twigs out of his
hair, then looked up at her again. "Well, are you
coming or what? I swear, it takes more work to get
you two going on a simple shopping trip than one
man can bear to handle."

Muttering under her breath, she started back
along the limb. Only one of her footholds didn't
hold so well. She heard the sharp crack of the small
limb and, though she grabbed hold of another, her
hands slipped over the smooth bark and she was
plummeting earthward almost before she knew it.

She didn't even have time to shriek.

And then she was in those big arms, just as her
son had been moments before. And Luke was looking down at her, his eyes surprised, then amused.
His chest was supporting her, his arms under her
shoulders and legs, holding her against him. So
every time he breathed, she felt herself rise and fall

with it. And his face was so close she could see the light shadow of stubble peeking out of his skin.

"You can put me down now."

"I can?" The words were muttered and not a real question. Then he caught himself, blinked and said, "Oh, right, sure," and set her on her feet.

Baxter was sitting there staring from one of them to the other. And Jasmine suddenly felt a rush of guilt rising up in her chest. She didn't know why. She hadn't done anything, and it wasn't as if she had any intention of changing that. But logical or not, the guilt was there, and in force. She'd nearly kissed this man, or maybe he had nearly kissed her. She couldn't be sure which, but there had definitely been a kiss lingering in the air between them, waiting to be claimed. She'd nearly kissed a man in front of her son. Her Baxter. As if he weren't even there. As if he didn't matter.

Chapter 7

Okay, Luke thought. So she was like a she-bear guarding a cub when it came to that boy of hers. Jasmine had clambered up the tree so all-fired fast that Luke hadn't even had time to offer to do it for her. Much less to suggest that might not be the safest course of action she could take. He had never seen anything like it. She hadn't even paused to think it over, just leaped onto the first branch she could reach and scuttled up so easily it would have made a mama chimp jealous of her skill.

Damn.

She loved the kid. Luke had already deduced that much. Hell, he *knew* she loved the kid. But in case there had been any room for doubt—in case he'd been thinking her overprotectiveness had some

other cause, like anal-retentive disorder or something—he now knew better. She might be a lot of
things, but chief among them was one: she was a
devoted mother. And that was something he
couldn't help but admire.

In all his life, as a kid like Baxter, with a mom
like Jasmine, he had never ever once doubted that
his mother loved him. That she would step in front
of a speeding train for him without batting an eye.
Even though she'd kept him from a lot of things—
like close friends, extended family, a peer group—
even though she'd smothered him to the point
where he'd nearly grown up to be an isolated, cut-
off loner of a man—he'd loved his mother. When
he'd lost her, for a while he'd been lost himself. If
he hadn't come here, found this big warm family...

Well, hell, it didn't pay much to think on what
might have been.

Jasmine rode beside Baxter and Luke in the
pickup that had been parked in back, out of sight,
bouncing in her seat with every pothole they hit.
She looked a bit more ''Quinn'' than she had when
she'd first arrived. She'd gone lighter on the
makeup by about a pound and a half, he guessed.
And the hair wasn't quite so big now. Still full and
fluffy, and soft as a dark silk cloud, but not as over
the top as before. And the jeans and T-shirt looked
good. Damn, they looked good, and he wasn't quite
sure why. They weren't tight, but slightly loose.
She just was one of those women he figured would

look good in anything, including a feed sack. However, those ridiculous talons of hers, with their gemstones winking, were still in place. And those shoes! God, where did she shop, at some dominatrix supply store? The heels were like vampire stakes, sharpened up for business. How did a person *walk* in those things?

"You might miss a few of these Texas-sized potholes if you'd quit staring at me and keep your eyes on the road," she told him, her tone a little sharp.

He glanced from her feet to her face. No amount of makeup could hide those big brown eyes now that he'd noticed them. Doe eyes. He felt as if he might fall into them before he managed to jerk his gaze back to the road. "I was wondering how you manage to walk in those shoes," he said, to make conversation.

"One step at a time, cowboy. Just like everybody else."

He glanced sideways at her, saw her lips quirk in a slight smile and knew she was teasing him a little. He didn't say any more, but sent Baxter, who sat between them, a wink.

A short while later he pulled the pickup to a stop. "This looks like a good place to start," he said. "What do you think, Baxter?"

Bax glanced through the windshield, and his eyes lit up when he spotted the giant ice-cream cone on top of the small log building.

Jasmine rolled her eyes. "Hell, you're just determined to make me fat, aren't you?"

Luke shrugged. "I'm guessin' you could eat nonstop for about a week and still have a ways to go for that, woman."

She smiled at him suddenly. Right out of the blue. "Thank you."

"Shoot, that was no compliment. Why do you city girls always take being malnourished as a good thing? You're downright scrawny." He looked at Baxter. "I say we get her a triple scoop super mocha sundae with extra whipped cream."

"Yeah!" Baxter said, giggling.

Jasmine was glowering at Luke again. "I'll have a soda," she said. "Diet."

"Darn. Looks like Bax will have to eat that sundae, then."

Bax laughed as if he would bust a gut, and Jasmine's glower eased away. Maybe she was starting to understand that he was kidding here, trying to keep Baxter's mind off his troubles.

He thought so even more when Jasmine ordered a small cone with a chocolate dip. They ate at one of the umbrella shaded picnic tables outside. He got momentarily lost in watching Jasmine eat ice cream. It was suitable fodder for the Playboy Channel, he figured. Or maybe it was just him. When they finished, he hauled them all over to the Wal-Mart, found a parking spot and stopped the truck.

Jasmine looked at the store, then sent Luke a doubtful glance.

"Anything you could possibly want or need, this is the place you'll find it," Luke promised her. "Hair care, clothes, shoes, even groceries. Knock yourself out."

"If you say so." She drew a breath and reached for Baxter's hand.

"Jasmine?" Luke said, and she looked back at him. He made his eyes as sincere as he could. "Why don't you let Baxter hang with me while you get your shopping done? I just have a few errands in town. Heck, I take Bubba with me all the time. Sometimes for the whole weekend, and he hasn't once gone home with so much as a mosquito bite."

She bit her lower lip. Luke noticed it, then made himself stop noticing it. "I don't know..." she said. Which meant she was wavering.

"You said you had a lot to do. And you know it'll be easier without him in tow. I promise, I won't let him out of my sight, not even for a second."

"Please, Mom?" Baxter asked.

She met Luke's eyes again, and he saw her message clearly. Let anything happen to my boy and I will kill you slowly. But aloud she said, "Oh, all right."

Bax squealed with delight and clapped his hands together. But while he celebrated, Jasmine reached out, and her slender hand, with its deadly nails, locked around Luke's arm with surprising strength.

"It's important you keep that promise about not letting him out of your sight," she told him, her voice very low. "Very important. And if you see any strangers paying him undue attention, get him out of there. Watch him, Luke."

The way she said it, the intensity in her eyes and the pressure of her hand on his arm...all those things combined delivered a message he would have preferred not to have received. The kid was in danger. Or Jasmine believe him to be. So those "bad guys" Baxter had mentioned twice were not just unpleasant characters or casual enemies, were they?

What the hell was going on with these two?

Too late to ask. She released him, leaned down to kiss her son's face and got out of the truck. "You be good, Baxter. You stay close to Luke, you hear?"

"I'll be good, Mom. Really."

An hour later Jasmine emerged from the store, her arms loaded down with shopping bags. She'd cashed both her own paycheck and Rosebud's on her way out of Illinois, so cash wasn't a problem. Not yet, anyway. As she entered the store, she practically bumped into a woman she didn't know. The woman had a baby on her hip. Jasmine muttered an apology, but the woman only stepped back, looked at her closely, and then smiled and said, "You must be Jasmine!"

Jasmine frowned, going on instant alert. "How do you know who I am?"

She was a pretty thing, with a Lois Lane look about her, and her baby was utterly gorgeous. Fat cheeks, blond curls. A little boy, six or seven months old, by Jasmine's best guess, wearing a tiny baseball cap with his jumper. The woman went right on speaking. "You're new in town. You're shopping right where my cousin said you'd be shopping. And of course, there are the nails. They clinched it."

"Not the nails again," Jasmine muttered, relaxing a bit as it hit her this must be yet another Brand.

"They're gorgeous," the woman said. "Let me take a few of those for you." She helped herself to three of Jasmine's bags, holding them in one hand and her baby in the other arm. "I'm Penny. My husband Ben is Garrett's brother. And this is Zachary, our son."

"He's adorable," Jasmine said, looking at the bright eyes that stared right back at her. The baby smiled and cooed. Then Jasmine said, "Did Luke send you here, then?"

"Uh-huh. He said to pick you up. He and Baxter, your own adorable little fellow, will meet you at the dojo in a bit. Okay?"

Jasmine shrugged. "Fine, I guess." She walked with Penny Brand out to her car, which turned out to be a hulking four-wheel-drive SUV in a pretty shade of forest-green. They stashed the bags in the back and the baby in the car seat, then got into the front.

As she fastened her seat belt, Penny said, "By the way, welcome to Quinn. I can't tell you how glad I am to meet you. It's like fate sent you along at the perfect time."

Jasmine frowned. "Why would you say that?"

Penny shrugged, turning the wheel, expertly pulling into the light traffic of town. "Baxter tells me you're a dancer."

"Um, yeah." She wondered if Luke had elaborated on that, if he'd told his cousin-in-law that she danced, all right—at a strip joint in the seedy part of Chicago.

"I think that is so incredible. God, I've always wished I could dance. I just seem to have two left feet. Were you formally trained or self-taught?"

So Luke hadn't told her the rest. Hell, he must be a throwback. You could only fake so much— she didn't think you could fake the kind of...chivalry, or whatever antiquated moral value prevented him from spilling her secrets to his family. And glancing at Penny, she saw yet another woman who seemed kind, friendly, genuinely interested in her, and not sporting any ulterior motives. She was beginning to think it didn't make a lot of sense to believe every single person she met was an incredibly talented actor, trying to snow her, up to no good.

My God, could these people genuinely be this nice?

"I, um…Chicago School of Dance," she said finally. "For three years. I worked two jobs to pay my tuition. But I had to drop out when Bax came along."

"Wow," Penny said, looking a little awed now. "You must be incredible. You're more than I could have hoped for." She seemed to be battling a full-blown face-splitting smile.

"Hoped for…for what?"

"Oh, just let me show you around the place first. We'll talk more after."

Jasmine studied the woman curiously as Penny drove into a parking lot and cut the engine. She glanced into the back. "Anything perishable back there?"

"No, nothing."

"Great. Let's go in then." She hopped out of the car, whipped open the back door and gathered up her baby. Then she headed toward the entrance of the large building.

It looked to Jasmine like a big old warehouse of some kind. Ribbed metal siding, a white metal roof. But the giant sign across the peak in front read The Dojo Spiritual Fitness Center, and underneath that, in slightly smaller script, Karate, Tae Kwon-Do, Tai Chi, Chi Gung, Yoga, Meditation.

As they walked toward the entrance, she wondered if Luke's cousin Ben looked anything like

David Carradine. Then she thought to glance around the parking lot. "I don't see Luke's truck," she said. She opened the door, holding it for Penny.

"Oh, he'll be along," she said, coming inside with the baby.

Inside, the place was even more impressive. Hardwood floors, stacks of mats, sliding walls that could divide the huge space into four separate rooms at will, and the walls...the walls had long, elegant dragons painted on them in brilliant reds, oranges and purples.

"Come on in, please," Penny said. "It's just as well no one's here right now. Maybe I can convince you to indulge me just a little bit."

"I don't follow."

But Penny was already rushing through the place, pointing this way and that. "That little room beyond the Plexiglas window is where the controls are for the sound system, the lighting, the divider walls, etc. It doubles as an office. The other doors over there are the rest rooms, and that final one leads upstairs. The entire second floor of the place is where we live."

"Wow. Must be tons of room."

"Oh, there is. I'll show you around up there later, if you like." She pulled a mat from the stack near the wall and set the baby down on it. Then she dipped into her purse for a handful of baby toys and put them down in front of him. Zachary grinned and gurgled and sat up by himself, then reached for his toys. "That's a good baby," Penny said. She left him and walked the four steps into the control room and office, and a second later Jasmine heard strains of music wafting from unseen speakers.

Penny came back out again, smiling. "Will you show me just a little?" she asked.

Jasmine frowned, then she got it. "You want me to dance?"

"I know it sounds silly, but, oh, please, I really do have a reason for asking. And I've loved dance all my life. And it's just you and me here, after all. Please?"

Jasmine shrugged. "To tell you the truth, it's been killing me not to have time to dance in the past few days—or a gym to practice in." She glanced behind her toward the door. The music was seeping into her muscles, making them twitch with longing. "Back in Chicago there was a gym right around the corner from the apartment. Rosebud and I used to go every day while Bax was at school. Kept us in shape, you know? I mean, it isn't like we had the chance to use our classical training much any other time...."

She found herself stretching as she spoke. Falling into her old patterns automatically, almost feeling as if Rosebud were with her, right now. In that old gym with the smelly locker room, their cheap boom box plugged into a wall socket, sitting on the floor. A handful of boys usually waiting for the room to free up so they could shoot hoops, heckling them.

She and Rosebud giving it right back. Then dancing
until those mouthy punks were just gaping, awe-
struck.

And then she was dancing. It came to her as nat-
urally as breathing. She let herself forget everything
that had happened. For a brief time she was back
there in that smelly gym around the corner. And
Rosebud was with her, dancing in perfect synch.
Closing her eyes, Jasmine gave herself over to the
music, let it bend and move her body with its notes
and rhythms. Moving her arms in graceful arcs.
Dancing was her sweetest release—her haven
where no hurt could get in. She lost herself completely to the music, to the dance, forgetting her
audience of one woman and one baby. Forgetting
the violence she had come here to escape. Forgetting everything, she danced.

Luke and Ben walked up to the front door of the
dojo and heard music. "Guess they got bored waiting for us," Ben said.

Luke smiled at him, glancing down at the boy
attached to the small hand that had been nestled
inside his larger one for most of the afternoon now.
He liked that feeling a little bit too much. He knew
he shouldn't let himself get as fond of Baxter as
this, feel as protective of him as he did. He
shouldn't get a little soft spot in his chest every time
those round wire-rimmed glasses slid down the
kid's nose. It was not a good idea to get this at-

tached to a child like Bax, with a mother like Jasmine. She wouldn't like it. She would probably rebel violently against it. He knew that instinctively. Moms like Jasmine didn't like other people getting close to their sons.

But that thought—along with every other coherent thought he might have had—abandoned his brain when he stepped into the dojo and saw her. At first he didn't fully comprehend. Had Ben finally hired a professional dance instructor for that class Penny wanted to add to the selection here? But what would a dancer this good be doing in a backwater town like Quinn?

And then he realized what his gut had known from the first glance. That dancer was Jasmine. She swirled and dipped, and when her arms moved they were liquid. Her hair flew when she whirled, and she moved faster and faster until she was only a blur in his eyes. And finally she stopped, ending bent low, almost hugging herself, her breaths rushing in and out in short, shallow puffs and her skin damp and glowing.

For some reason, Garrett's words floated into his mind. "You're doomed, cuz." And he thought maybe he was. That was it for him—the moment when he walked in and saw her dancing. He didn't want it to be. But he saw now that he'd never had much choice in the matter. Otherwise, what was the heavy object that nailed him in the chest like a two-by-four just now?

Luke heard clapping. He blinked out of the stupor her dance had evoked in him and looked around. Ben was there, clapping slowly along with Penny. On the floor, wide-eyed, little Zachary grinned and copied them, smacking his tiny hands together repeatedly. Baxter clapped, too, louder and harder than anyone else.

Jasmine lifted her head, eyes wide in surprise. Her eyes seemed to find Luke's as if by radar, and then she lowered her gaze. Her face was already flushed with heat and exertion, but Luke thought it got even redder. Was she blushing? And how much sense did that make? She danced half-naked for men for a living. How could dancing this way, in front of him, fully clothed, make her blush?

"I told you my mom was the best dancer in the world!" Baxter said, his little chest puffing out.

"You sure did, Bax," Luke said.

"That was incredible," Penny said through her smile. "Incredible! Wasn't it, Ben?"

"Blew me away," Ben said. "Okay, Penny, you win."

Penny looked at him, brows rising high. "I get to have my dance class?"

He nodded. "Can't deprive the Quinn kids of learning something that powerful, now can we? And as for the teacher, well, we couldn't top what I've just seen here if we advertised for six months. If Jasmine wants the job, it's hers."

Penny clapped her hands together. Everyone was

smiling. Everyone, Luke noticed, except for Jasmine. She was still staring at him, and it hit him that maybe she was waiting for him to make some comment about what he'd seen just now. Everyone had raved about her dancing except for him, and, uh, little Zachary on the floor there. Although at least the little one had clapped and drooled. Anyway, before he could find words, Jasmine looked away from him, as if Ben's words had finally registered.

"What job?" she asked.

"I want to add dance classes to our schedule, for the local kids," Penny said. "I have almost fifty parents interested already. But I couldn't do it without a qualified teacher, and I just didn't know where to find one." She smiled. "Until now."

Jasmine sent a swift glance toward Luke yet again. It took a moment before it dawned on him what she was waiting for. She was expecting him to inform his cousins what kind of dancing she had been doing up until recently. To tell them that they wouldn't want a woman like her teaching ballet and the like to young impressionable kids.

"I really...don't think I'm...qualified," Jasmine said at last.

Luke swallowed hard. "You're right. You're not. What you're qualified for is dancing on some Paris stage while people throw roses at your feet."

Those big brown eyes went wider. Her lips

pulled slightly, and she lowered her head. "You know better than that Luke."

"No, I don't. I've never seen anything like that before, Jasmine. And I already know how wonderful you are with kids. So I'd say you're more than qualified to take this job on, if you want it. And...if you're planning to stay around Quinn awhile."

"Are you?" Penny asked.

"Are we, Mom?" Baxter echoed.

Luke looked at Baxter's hopeful expression and wondered how much his own mirrored it. He tried to school himself into a less obvious countenance, but he couldn't help hoping she would say yes.

Jasmine looked from one of them to the other and, sighing, closed her eyes. "I don't know. I'm sorry, I just...I don't know."

Being in Quinn, Texas, at night was as different from being in Chicago as being on another planet would be. It wasn't the sounds, or the lack of them. Or the smells, or the lack of *them*. It was the feeling. A safe, secure, utterly fictional feeling that all was right with the world. People who lived in small towns were seriously deluded. Lulled into believing in the spell places like this could cast.

Baxter was tucked safely in Luke Brand's big bed, sound asleep already. Jasmine sat outside on the porch swing, rocking slowly, breathing honeysuckle-laden night air and listening to the endless chorus of background music. Coyotes warbling their sad, lonely cries. Cicadas chirping madly. The distant moan of the wind. Above her, beyond the porch roof, were stars. She didn't think she had ever seen so many stars in the sky in her life. They spread like a twinkling blanket over the world.

The creak of the screen door and heavy footfalls spoke of Luke's approach even before he sat down beside her on the swing. He gave a push of his big boots and sent the thing into greater arcs than before. Then he crossed his arms behind his head and leaned back, stretching out his long legs.

"It's pretty here, isn't it?" he said. "Prettiest place I think I've ever seen. And I've seen a lot of places."

"It's pretty here," she agreed. "Can't argue with that."

"This place—it's part of what made me decide to stop running, put down some roots."

"I suppose it's as good a place as any to settle down."

"Nope," he said. "Better."

She lifted her brows. "Look, if you're trying to sell me on that job offer of Penny's—"

"Jasmine, I know something's wrong." He stopped the swing, sat up straighter and turned partway around to face her. "I know you're scared, but you've got to stop running sometime. Some*where.* Sooner or later, you have to turn around and fight this thing, whatever it is, or it'll dog you to the end of your days."

She averted her eyes. He was far more perceptive than she wanted him to be. "What makes you think I'm running from anything?"

He looked at her, his expression telling her not to even bother with the denial. "Sooner or later," he said again, "you gotta stand and fight. For Baxter's sake, if not your own."

She shook her head hard. "It's for Baxter's sake I have to keep running."

He paused a beat, maybe digesting that. Then he said, "Tell me what it is."

"I can't."

Pursing his lips, he nodded. "Okay, you can't. It doesn't matter what it is, anyway, because eventually it'll catch up to you. Here...*here* is where you have the best shot at beating it. Better than any other place where you might run out of time. Here, Jasmine. You can win here."

Lifting her gaze slowly, she searched his eyes. "What makes here so much different than anywhere else?"

He pinned her with a piercing stare. "I'm here."

She wished with everything in her that she could believe him. But she couldn't. She couldn't risk Baxter's life on the word of a man who was little more than a stranger to her. Sooner or later Petronella would track her down, and she needed to make sure she and Bax were gone before that happened. God, if he caught up to her here, Luke and his entire family would be at risk. That thought gave her pause. Since when did she worry about outsiders? It had been her and Baxter and, until recently, Rosebud, against the world.

And yet a part of her was beginning to care about these people. And a part of her longed to stay in a place like this. To take the job Ben and Penny had offered, teaching dance to children. God, it would be so much better than what she'd been doing for a living up to now. And living in a town like this one—with people like these, who, honest to God, seemed to care about others more than they did about themselves—would be heaven. For her, and especially for Baxter. Already Baxter's cheeks had a healthier glow to them than they'd ever had before. And he'd laughed out loud more in the time they'd spent here than he normally did in a whole week.

God, it would be perfect here.

If only it could be.

She stared back at Luke, unable to look away from that penetrating stare, and the next thing she knew, he was kissing her. His mouth pressed to hers, his arms slid gently around her. It wasn't the sloppy, groping sort of kiss men occasionally forced on her when they caught her alone in the parking lot after a show. This was different. Fleeting and tender. His hands gently cupped the back of her head, as his lips tasted hers lightly, softly.

Her breath sighed out slowly, and her body softened. And then he let her go.

She sat there reeling, wondering what the hell that meant or what he wanted or what she was supposed to do now.

But then a gut-wrenching scream shattered the night's song, chasing all those questions from her mind as she came to her feet in a single heartbeat. "Baxter!" she cried.

Chapter 8

"It's okay, baby. Hush, now, it's okay. Shh."

Her voice was like the wind, its soothing, healing song so gentle that it didn't matter what she said. It was the way she said it as she held little Baxter close to her, rocking him back and forth.

His nightmare had been a bad one. Luke could see that plainly in the boy's paler-than-normal face and sweat-damp hair. He'd rushed into the room on Jasmine's heels when the child had cried out, flicked on the light instantly, instinctively. Now he felt useless, standing there, watching Jasmine magically drive the fear away from her little boy with her embrace and her soft, calming voice. "It was only a dream, Bax. Only a dream. It wasn't real. Mama's right here. I won't let anything hurt you. You know that."

The child clung to her, trembling still, but nodding against her shoulder. Her hands moved over his small back in soothing circles, patting now and then but mostly rubbing. Where did mothers learn that? Luke wondered. Was there some kind of instruction manual that came with kids, or what? The woman was a master.

Sniffling, Baxter sat away from her a little, rubbed at his cheek with the back of his hand. "Can I have some warm milk?"

"You can have anything you want, baby."

Finally seeing something he could do, Luke came to attention. "I'll get it."

Jasmine turned as if she'd forgotten he was there. "No, I have to do it."

Luke lifted his brows. Baxter sniffled and said, "No one else knows how to do it the way Mom does."

"Oh. All right, then."

Jasmine looked at him as she got to her feet, and he could see the worry in her eyes. The tension. And no wonder. His own heart was only just beginning to return to a normal rate. As she passed him, she reached up, closed her small hand on his arm. "Would you stay with Bax while I get that milk?"

He glanced down at her, touching him like that. He wasn't sure she'd even thought about it first. He wasn't sure if it meant anything, or if it was just a reflexive action. For the first time since hearing the boy's scream, he let himself review what had happened just prior to it. That kiss on the porch swing, under the stars. What the hell had that been about? He hadn't meant to kiss her. Hadn't planned to kiss her. It just sort of…happened. And he didn't know what it meant to him, much less what she might be making of it in her mind. Did that touch have anything to do with the kiss? And if so, what?

Her hand was still on his arm. Experimentally he covered her hand with his own. "I'll be right here. Don't worry, Bax will be fine till you get back."

Lifting her gaze to his, she seemed a bit startled but more comforted. "You want me to bring you some warm milk, too?"

He shook his head left, then right. It was going to take a lot more than warm milk to help him get to sleep tonight, he thought vaguely. A hell of a lot more. For some reason he had a foolish image in his head—one of him sitting in a chair beside the bed, watching over the two of them while they slept. As if that would do any good. He couldn't very well keep their nightmares away.

He reached up in spite of himself and tucked her hair behind her ear. "Yell if you need any help with that milk."

She nodded and left the room.

Luke sighed as he watched her go. He *really* didn't want to be drawn to her the way he was. He'd tried to tell Garrett having her here with him wasn't a good idea. Damn his oversize meddling cowboy cousin, anyway. What the hell was he going to do with a woman like her? He'd barely survived the first overprotective woman in his life, why on earth would he want to take up with another one?

She was totally opposite from the kind of woman he thought he might want to settle down with someday. And besides, that someday was still a long way off. This whole "sell the truck, buy the ranch, put down roots" experiment was barely underway. He had no idea if he could be a settling-down kind of man. Suppose it turned out his mother had been right all along? Suppose he'd inherited his father's wanderlust? What then? This woman needed more than that. Hell, Baxter needed more than that. He didn't think he had enough love in him to heal the wounds he saw in these two wayfarers.

"Luke?"

He turned to look at Bax in the big bed, looking small and alone. "Yeah, pal?"

"I'm scared, Luke."

A tiny arrow slid right into his heart, and Luke went to the bed and sat down on the side. "It's okay to be scared. Just so you know you're not alone. I'm here, and your mom, too."

"But what if they find us?"

Luke drew his brows together. "What if who find you? Are you talking about your dream, Bax? 'Cause, you know, dreams aren't real."

"This one was. I dreamed of those men, back in

Chicago. The big one, he had a gun. And he shot that other man with it, and I saw! And then he tried to shoot me, and when Mommy made him stop, he tried to shoot her.'' He lowered his head, great big tears rolling down his face. "And I think he got Aunt Rosebud. That's why she had to go live with the angels.''

He curled into Luke's arms, wrapped his small ones around Luke's neck and rested his face on his chest, while Luke sat there stunned right to his bones. "I'm so afraid those men will find us. What if they hurt Mom the way they hurt Aunt Rosebud? What if I lose her, too?''

"Hey. You look at me, pal.'' Luke drew Baxter's chin up and stared right into his eyes. "I promise you, I'm not gonna let anyone hurt you. Or your mom. You got that? Any bad guy tries to get near the two of you, he's gonna have to go through me and my whole family first. Now, you've only met a few of us. Bubba and Garrett and Chelsea, Ben and Penny and Zach. But there's a bunch more. There's Wes, Taylor, Adam, Kirsten, Elliot, Esmeralda, Lash and Jessi—oh, there's a pile of us Brands around here.''

"There are?'' The boy looked up, wide-eyed, trusting but doubtful.

"Wait…I have a picture,'' Luke said. "We took one of the whole clan at the big family picnic a month ago.''

Luke got up, only to his surprise, the little fellow

clung like a burr—arms and legs wrapped tight. He carried Bax with him to the dresser, opened a drawer and reached in for the photo album he kept there. He was startled to feel soft, lacy, silky things brushing over his hands. Jasmine, it seemed, had commandeered some drawer space. And though his throat went dry as a bone, he ignored them and located the album.

Then he sat down on the bed with the boy on his lap and flipped pages until he found the photo. The eight-by-ten took up the entire page. "There now, see that?" Seventeen adults and three children were in that photo. The entire surviving Brand clan. Well, the legitimate branch of it, anyway. The Oklahoma wing of the family hadn't been present. "Most of the folks in this picture are within shouting distance, you know. This one here is Marcus. He's my half brother. And that cute one, there in the front, that's Sara, my half sister. You know I only met them a couple months ago?"

"Really?"

"Mmm-hmm. They live close by, down near El Paso. It's not far. And let me tell you what they told me when I first found all these relatives of mine. 'Luke,' they said. 'When one member of this family gets into trouble, every single Brand in Texas drops whatever they're doing and hightails it to them to help them out. Doesn't matter where they are, or what the trouble is. That's just the way this family works.'"

Baxter stared up at him, big brown eyes starting to look sleepy. "But I'm not part of the family."

"Well, heck, Baxter, you're livin' with me, aren't you?"

"Yeah...."

"Well, that makes you part of the family in my book. Besides, that's the other thing about this family. If they like you, they tend to want to make you an honorary Brand."

"They do?"

"Oh, heck yeah. So you might as well consider yourself in. I doubt they'd listen even if you tried to tell 'em you didn't want to be. 'Specially Bubba. He's been itching for a cousin big enough for him to hang out with."

Baxter smiled wider than Luke had ever seen him, hugged Luke tight and then crawled under the covers, taking the photo album with him. He curled up with it clasped to his chest and closed his eyes. "Thanks, Luke," he said. "I never had a real family before—'cept for Mom and Aunt Rosebud. I think I like having one this big."

His throat so dry he could scarcely speak, Luke rasped, "Me too."

Jasmine stood in the doorway, the milk with a touch of honey and a bit of strong chamomile tea mixed in, warmed to just the right temperature, in her hands. The scene in the bedroom looked like the artwork from some sentimental Father's Day card. Luke sat on the edge of the bed, and Baxter lay in it, but he'd curled around Luke like a cat. And as he lay there sound asleep, Luke's oversize hand ran slowly over Baxter's dark blond hair, again and again.

The sight of her son with a man in such an affectionate way was totally foreign to Jasmine. And totally unexpected. She didn't think she liked it very much. A dark wave of something that felt a little bit like petty jealousy sloshed against her heart. She chased it away and told herself that was foolish, that her main concern had to be Baxter. And that for him to get attached to this cowboy, who could only be a temporary guest in their lives, would be a big mistake. Come to think of it, that might be a good thing for her to remember herself. She could easily get hurt. More importantly, Bax could get hurt.

From the looks of things, so might Luke. He was not, she finally admitted to herself, acting a part. He was genuine.

Jasmine sighed, lowering her gaze. "I think he's out cold, Luke," she whispered.

He turned toward her, then sent her a lopsided smile that told her she was too late to save him. Her Baxter had worked himself into the big guy's heart already. Carefully Luke eased himself off the bed and out of Baxter's clutches. Once on his feet, he bent to tuck the blankets around Baxter, and when he came toward the door, Jasmine reached for the light switch.

Luke's hand covered hers, closed around it and pulled it gently away. "Why don't you leave it on for him?"

She frowned but left the light on. They stepped into the hall together, and Luke pulled the door closed, but not all the way closed. Then he tiptoed along the hall to the stairs and down them. Only when they were in the living room did he speak at something approaching a normal volume. Taking a seat on the sofa, he said, "When I was a kid, I was scared to death of the dark. My mom thought it would make me weak to leave the light on for me. So she would just shut it off, close the door up tight and leave me there alone. Said it would cure me."

Jasmine lifted her brows. "Did it?"

He shook his head. "I was still fighting it into my teens. And suffering from too little sleep all the while in between." He shrugged. "Course, having that bright light on all night isn't the solution either. But I was thinking, we could maybe pick him up a night-light tomorrow. I mean—if it's okay with you. You're his mom, after all."

She nodded slowly. "Fine by me." Then she sighed. "I'd never make him sleep in the dark if he was afraid. It's just...he's never been afraid before."

Luke nodded, and she felt his eyes probing her

closely. "Seems like something happened to make him afraid."

She looked up sharply. What had Baxter told him?

"And you're afraid, too," he said. "At first I thought you were just overprotective, and you are, to a point. But it's not just that."

"I'm not overprotective."

"Yeah, you are. I know. I had a mother just like you."

She narrowed her eyes, opened her mouth to speak, but he held up a hand. "Don't get defensive, Jasmine. You're a fine mother to that boy. Any fool could see that. I'm not arguing it. I got off the subject."

"The subject being?" she asked.

"What the hell happened in Chicago? I mean, damn, woman, I knew there was something dogging you. I thought it was a man, a bad relationship, a custody battle, something like that. But now..."

She went stiff. So Baxter had told him something after all.

"Jasmine, Baxter's troubles here are a damn sight bigger than fear of the dark or a scraped-up knee, and we both know it."

She licked her lips, averting her eyes. She should go up to bed. She should walk away. "What makes you think so?"

He sighed in exasperation, lifting his palms.

"Come on, Jasmine, will you quit with this? Baxter says someone tried to shoot him and you!"

"He just had a nightmare."

"No wonder. Sounds like you've been living one lately."

"Look, I can't talk about this."

He said nothing for so long she had to lift her eyes and meet his steady gaze. Finally he just sighed. "Sooner or later you're going to have to trust someone, Jasmine. If someone's after you, I can help. And I will. But I can't if you don't tell me what's going on."

He waited. Jasmine stared at the floor, gnawed her lip and almost considered telling him the truth. But no, she couldn't do that, for so many reasons. First and foremost, because it would mean admitting she had no legal right to be staying in this house. She didn't really think he would toss her out if he knew that, but he could. And besides, one of the men after her was a cop. This man's cousin, Garrett, was a cop, too. How could she be sure they would believe her over that murdering bastard in Chicago? Sure, they might take her word for things at first—but when it came to her word against that of a police officer, that might change.

She squirmed inwardly. It was so ingrained in her not to trust, not to accept help from outsiders, not to let anyone in. And yet she'd never wanted to, felt driven to do just that, the way she did now. With this man. This family. But beyond all that lay one simple, dark truth that made the rest moot. Telling Luke and the Brands would add them to the list of targets to be silenced.

She didn't want to rain that kind of disaster down on this family. She'd stirred up enough of a whirlwind in their lives already.

Luke was still looking at her, still waiting. She lifted her gaze to his.

He saw her answer in her eyes, because he sighed and said, "Sooner or later, Jasmine, you're gonna trust me enough to open up to me." He offered her a small smile, one meant to be comforting, she was sure. "But for now...maybe you could just let me taste that special warm milk you make like no one else in the known universe?"

Her tense muscles uncoiled slowly, and if the breath rushed out of her in relief, well, she couldn't help that. She held up the glass, and he took it, sipped it, smacked his lips and wore a milk mustache. "Mmm. Bax was right."

"It's just milk and honey, with a little touch of chamomile."

He drank some more, then handed her the glass. "Finish it up, hon. You're gonna have trouble sleeping, too, after all this."

Hon. She didn't think anyone had called her that since Rosebud. It made her throat get tight and her eyes burn. He saw it, damn him. And though she sipped the milk to cover her pain, he didn't stop seeing it. She could feel him seeing it. When she set the glass down, he smiled, and reached up to brush her upper lip with his thumb. And then his eyes got darker, somehow. And he leaned closer and kissed her. It was soft, light, gentle. And when he lifted his head away, he licked his lips, tasting that milk and honey, she knew, because she'd tasted it on him, as well.

"I've been thinking about kissing you ever since I walked in and saw you dancing today."

Her brows bent until they touched. "Why?"

"Why?" He shook his head. "Because it was beautiful. You were…I've never known anyone who could move like that. It was like…music. Yeah. If music could move, that's what it would look like."

She blinked. She didn't think she'd ever been given such a sincere compliment before. "You thought all I could do was bump and grind?"

He checked her face quickly, as if looking to make sure she wasn't getting defensive on him. She couldn't blame him for that. She tended to get defensive where her work was concerned. She smiled a little. "It's okay. Most people don't expect strippers to have a hell of a lot of talent. But I was classically trained. It's just not a very efficient way to earn a living, is all. I had a child to feed."

He shook his head. "You don't have to explain yourself to me."

"I know." She looked at him, studied his blue eyes. "But for some asinine reason, I want to. I've never felt ashamed of dancing for a living, Luke. Expressing emotions through dance, even emotions like passion or lust, is an art. Exotic dancing has a long history. Even a sacred one. I mean, the first striptease was The Dance of the Seven Veils, you know. And it was first performed by a goddess. It's not the dancers who should feel shame for what they do. Not if they do it well. It's the men who watch them. I mean, they have a choice, too. They can react with a stirring of desire, with appreciation and admiration and pleasure. Or they can shout obscenities and try to cop a feel at every opportunity. Either way, it doesn't change the quality of the dance.''

He tipped his head to one side, then averted his eyes. "I never thought of it that way.''

"No. Most men don't.'' She looked at him, then looked again. His face was redder than before. His neck, too. "It's embarrassing you, talking about this, isn't it?''

He lifted his gaze. "No. That's not the word I would use.''

She looked closer. He looked away. "Maybe you should go on up to bed,'' he suggested, his voice a little raspy.

Frowning, still not able to read him, she said, "Oh. Well, okay.'' She got to her feet. Then she turned to look at him. "Thanks,'' she said. "For being so good to Baxter tonight.''

His face eased a bit, and he smiled. "How could I not be? The kid's a charmer."

"He is, isn't he?"

Luke nodded, but his eyes slid from hers to her lips, and then he lowered them to the floor again. "Good night, Jasmine," he said, and he said it like a dismissal.

She shrugged, not getting him. She could almost think he wanted her...except if he did, he would have tried something more than just the innocent little kisses he'd stolen. He would have been all over her by now if that were the case. Or...the men she'd known up to now would have, anyway.

Then again, she reminded herself, Luke was nothing like the men she'd known up to now. She didn't know what to make of a man like him. How to read him. "Good night, Luke."

She felt his eyes on her all the way up the stairs, though. And when she turned at the top to look down at him, she saw him staring hard and met his eyes and swore there was desire there. He held her gaze for a long moment, and then he finally turned away.

Jasmine went into the bedroom and climbed carefully under the covers to snuggle up with her little boy. She held her son and vowed to keep his nightmares away.

When Jasmine went to bed, she left her bag on the table. Luke picked it up, struggling to resist the urge to go through it for some clue as to what she was hiding. He managed, though. He carried it to the hook on the wall and hung it up. It swung heavily, and when it hit the wall there was a clunk. A metallic clunk. One that made his breath hitch in his chest and drew his gaze back to the handbag.

Frowning, he told himself that wasn't what it sounded like, and that the shape now visible in the bottom of the bag wasn't what it looked like, and that the weight in the bag wasn't what it felt like. But he stopped resisting, and he took the bag down off the peg and reached inside to make sure.

A cold metal handgun lay in the bottom. His hand bumped against it, then closed around it, and he pulled it out. "Ah, hell." He checked it, saw that it was unloaded. At least she wasn't totally insane. Glancing guiltily toward the stairs, and feeling justified now, he carried the bag to the sofa with him and, sitting down, began pulling out its contents, item by item.

His Jasmine had two identities, it seemed. She had one driver's license with her own pretty face on it. The name it listed was Jasmine Delaney Jones. And she had a second driver's license, this one with another woman's face on it. Her name, it said, was Jenny Lee Walker.

He closed his eyes. Damn. Just how much trouble was Jasmine in?

His stomach clenched again, as it had when her words earlier had his mind conjuring images of her dancing just for him. And that made him wonder how much trouble *he* was in.

Baxter came down for breakfast just as Luke finished pouring orange juice and set the glass down on the table. The boy looked at the cereal bowl and the assortment of boxes on the table, then sent Luke a quizzical glance. "But it's Sunday."

"Oh, yeah, that's right," Luke said. He refilled his coffee cup and took a seat opposite the boy. "And you usually have a big Sunday breakfast, don't you?"

Smiling, Baxter nodded.

"Well, to be honest, I always liked a big Sunday breakfast, too. But I learned pretty quick that it's a big mistake to fill up on Sunday morning around here."

Baxter tipped his head sideways. "Why?"

"Because every Sunday afternoon, the whole family heads over to the ranch for a giant barbeque."

"They do?"

"Sure they do. So I tend to eat light on Sunday mornings, just to save room for all the goodies in the afternoon. There's usually pie and ice cream for dessert. I always make sure I leave room for that."

"Wow." Baxter chose a box of cereal, poured, then paused and glanced at Luke. "Is it just for real Brands, or can 'on'ry ones go, too?"

Reaching across the table, Luke ruffled the kid's hair. "Honorary ones are our favorites."

Baxter grinned wider and added milk to his cereal.

Luke felt eyes on him and looked up. Jasmine stood in the archway, and he had no idea how long she'd been there or how much she'd heard. She'd obviously been up for a while, though. Her hair was done. No ponytail necessary. It had been washed and spritzed and blow-dried so that its curls fell in bunches over her shoulders. Her makeup was done, too. Not to the same extremes as that first time he'd seen her. But more than the light touch of yesterday. Any flaws in her skin were hidden, and her high cheekbones were accentuated; her eyes were lined and shadowed, and her lashes were thickened. And her lips...her lips were shiny and moist and pink, and he thought they looked tastier than anything his cousins might have to offer this afternoon.

"Can I talk to you for a second, Luke?"

He realized he'd been staring at her, taking stock of every difference in her this morning and wondering why a woman as beautiful as she was would be so merciless as to try to make herself even more irresistible. She wore a pair of snug-fitting jeans she must have picked up in town on their shopping trip, and a ribbed tank top that showed off her figure and her tan.

Nodding, he got to his feet. "Be right back, pal," he said to Baxter, and then he joined Jasmine in the archway. She led him into the living room, then turned to face him. "What are you doing, telling him he's an honorary Brand? Inviting him to family gatherings? What are you thinking?"

Her eyes were pained, her voice a harsh whisper.

"I...I just thought it would be fun for him, is all. He can play with Bubba and maybe ride a pony and—"

"He is *not* riding on any pony."

"Aw, come on, Jasmine. I wouldn't let him get hurt. You know that."

She stared into his eyes for so long he thought he could see her heartbeat, and then she finally turned away, sighing. "Dammit, Luke, why do you have to be so damned good to him? Making him breakfast. Taking him for ice cream. Treating him like family."

"What's so wrong with those things, Jasmine?"

She lifted her head fast. "You're teaching him that it's okay to depend on other people. You're making him lose his edge, Luke."

"Are we talking about Baxter now...or you?" Luke asked.

"You're making him love you," she whispered.

"So I'll ask you again, are we talking about Baxter...or—"

"It's gonna break his heart when we have to leave," she said, interrupting him before he could finish the sentence. And yet, he thought, the question still applied.

Luke put a hand on her shoulder. Her silky, soft skin against his calluses. The friction made his stomach clench. "Who says you have to leave?"

Her eyes widened before she turned away. "I do. Life does. We can't stay, Luke."

He frowned, turning her to face him. "What do you mean, you can't stay? You're challenging me for the house, aren't you? What are you gonna do, sell it and move on?"

She stared at him hard and finally lowered her head. "I'm not challenging you for the house. I just needed someplace safe for a few days, until I could figure out what to do." She lifted her gaze to his again. "I'm sorry I made you think you might lose the place. You're not going to. We couldn't stay here, even if we wanted to."

"Why not?"

She started to turn away, but he held both shoulders now, and he wouldn't let her. "Why not, Jasmine?" he asked again.

"Because sooner or later our past is going to catch up with us, and when it does, we have to move on."

"You can't run forever," he said.

"You just watch me." Again she turned away from him. This time he let her. He stood there, wondering what the hell to do, how to get her to open up to him…knowing damn well that if he kept pushing, she would bolt. Finally he sighed and said, "At least come to the ranch with me today. At least let Baxter enjoy himself for a little while. He'll have so much fun at the Texas Brand. And you can be there to watch him every second.''

He saw her lower her head, shake it slowly. ''You're as good at wheedling as he is, you know that?''

Luke shrugged. ''So will you come?''

''Yeah. We'll come.'' She turned and waggled a finger at him. ''But no pony rides.''

''Yes, ma'am.''

Several hours later, Luke sat astride one of Wes's prize Appaloosas, with Baxter cradled in the saddle in front of him. Jasmine looked on, gnawing her lip and regretting that she'd ever let the two of them talk her into this insanity, praying Bax wouldn't fall and get trampled underneath those giant hooves. Of course, Luke had a firm hold on him. And Baxter was laughing and smiling as if he'd never had so much fun in his life.

''Luke's great with him, isn't he?'' Chelsea asked.

They were sitting across from one another at one of the picnic tables on the big front lawn, sipping coffee. Jasmine was surrounded by more women than she was used to seeing in one place. Women usually didn't like her too much. She'd always assumed that was because they saw her as a threat. These women, however, seemed as if that were the least of their worries. And to Jasmine's surprise, not

one of their men had given her so much as a leering
look when his wife's back was turned. Not one.

She didn't think they made men like these guys
anymore. She was through doubting they were genuine, though.

Jessi, the Brand sister with the pixie short red
hair, perched on the railing. Taylor, the stunning
dark-skinned Comanche married to Wes Brand, sat
sideways on the top step with her back against the
railing and her belly looking like a beach ball in
her lap. Esmeralda, the sloe-eyed, slightly other-
worldly wife of Elliot, with her thick Spanish ac-
cent, was in a wicker rocker with her belly every
bit as swollen. They were a fertile bunch, these
Brands, Jasmine mused. Penny sat on a blanket in
the grass and watched Jessi's gorgeous toddler, Maria-Michelle, play gently with her own infant, Zachary.

Jasmine listened to their conversation. They
talked about their kids and their pets—Penny's family of bulldogs raced around with the kids like kids
themselves, while Bubba's aging hound dog, Blue,
observed with amused indulgence. They laughed
and joked, and exchanged lighthearted gossip. One
of the Loomis boys was getting married. The local
bar was adding a dining room. Maria-Michelle had
the sniffles.

The place spread out like some fairy-tale land
peopled with characters straight out of a fantasy.
Devoted husbands and loyal wives, happy families.

Horses and cattle and puppies racing to and fro. Big red barns and wide, rolling fields so green they hurt your eyes to look too long, underneath the biggest, bluest sky in all the world. For God's sake, there was even a tire swing in a tree out there in the distance! And a swimming hole "down back" she'd heard mentioned when the sun started beaming down hotter than before.

If someone had described this place, this scene, this family, to her before, she wouldn't have believed them. She would have called them a liar. She would have told them they'd been watching too much television. Damn, Rosebud would have loved this.

Of course, this family was sheltered here in this rural place. So far away from the touch of anything evil or dangerous. They wouldn't know what to do if they faced the kind of trouble haunting Jasmine and Baxter. They wouldn't have a clue.

Chelsea was getting up, waving now. "Come on, kids. Come get changed and we'll take you out to the pond to cool off, okay?"

Luke got off the big horse, lifting Baxter easily and setting him on the ground. Baxter came running, eyes huge, face pink with the sun and exertion. He honestly looked happier than she'd ever seen him. "Me too, Mom?"

Jasmine sent Luke a questioning look.

He gave her an imperceptible nod, and oddly, she found that was assurance enough for her. She was coming to trust the man, she realized with a start. If he said it was safe, she believed it. And that was just so odd it was like a *Twilight Zone* moment. She had to give her head a shake. This was all surreal. Was she dreaming this place? Was she dreaming *him?*

She didn't know. She would process all that later. For now, she took her son's hand and led him into the big farmhouse to help him change into the shorts Luke had insisted she bring along.

A short while later she was watching her son splash in a shallow frog pond with Bubba Brand, who seemed to have become his new best friend. And she realized it really was going to break Baxter's heart to leave here.

Why did life have to be so unfair?

Chapter 9

"So?" Garrett asked. He walked beside Luke, leading the horses the kids had been riding out to the stable.

"So, what?" Luke asked.

Behind him, the other men chuckled. And they were all there, too, following along for no good reason. Obviously this discussion was of interest to every macho Brand male in the county. Wes, the hot-tempered half Comanche. Elliot the redheaded jokester. Adam, the levelheaded *GQ* cover looka-like. And Lash, Garrett's deputy, even though he was a Brand by marriage, rather than blood. He'd married the baby sister of the family.

"So, has your houseguest told you anything about herself yet?"

Licking his lips, Luke stopped walking. The horse he'd been leading nickered and stomped a foot at him, impatient for the oats she knew awaited her in the stables, no doubt. Luke looked at the men. "I trust you guys like I've never trusted any man in my life except maybe for my old friend, Buck, whose death sort of led me to you all."

Wes lowered his head and reached up to clap Luke on the shoulder. Elliot grinned and shrugged, then said, "So what's not to trust?"

Luke shook his head. "I need to know you trust me the same way."

Ben bit his lower lip to hide a smile, and the other guys seemed to be battling the same. Garrett said, "You're falling for her already, huh?"

Luke swung his head around so fast he wrenched his neck. "What? No! I mean...not really. I...she..."

Garrett snorted, he was trying so hard not to laugh. Elliot reached up to smack Luke between the shoulder blades. "Just breathe, cuz. It's okay, it's happened to all of us."

Luke rolled his eyes. "There's nothing going on between the two of us."

"But you're attracted to her," Lash said, and it wasn't really even a question.

"Well, of course I'm attracted to her. I mean, have you *looked* at the woman? Who *wouldn't* be attracted to her? But that doesn't mean a damn thing. Hell, I'm not even sure I'm ready for a relationship with a woman. And even if I was, I'm not sure she'd be the one. She's sure as hell not what I had in mind.''

"Nope. They never are," Elliot said, shaking his head slowly.

"Doesn't matter if he's ready or not, anyway," Lash said. "Jessi made up her mind a good hour ago. She pulled me aside after the meal, said she thought Jasmine was perfect for Luke."

"Yeah, Chelsea thinks Jasmine and little Baxter fit into this family like missing puzzle pieces," Garrett said.

Elliot grinned at Luke. "Well, hell, cousin, that just about seals your fate, then. If Jessi and Chelsea want her in, she'll be in, and you're the only single male left to marry off to *get* her in."

Luke felt the blood drain from his face. *"Marry?"*

Lash nodded. "Shoot, they're probably picking out flowers by now."

Luke just stood there, feeling his head spin and his stomach lurch. And then they all burst out laughing. It was one big masculine roar, and so many hands slapped his back and shoulders that he figured he'd be bruised the next day.

Then Garrett was in his face. "Hey, don't look like that. We were only teasing you, Luke. Come on, don't faint on us."

He shook himself, shot Garrett a scowl. "I don't *faint.*" Then he led the mare the rest of the way to the stable, talking as he went. "Shoot, I wanted to talk to you guys about something important, and you all have to go off on me like a bunch of freaking...."

"Brothers?" Garrett asked when they got to the stable door. He pulled it open and led the horse inside. All the others trooped past, and Luke stood there looking in at them, a horse at his side.

"Yeah," he said with a grudging smile. "Yeah, that's exactly what you're acting like." He led the other horse inside, no longer angry. Then he held her while Wes rubbed her down.

"So what do you know about her?" Garrett asked.

Luke sighed. "That's what I wanted to talk about. She's in trouble, Garrett. And what I've found so far doesn't look good for her."

Garrett lifted his brows. "But you don't believe the evidence you're seeing?"

"No. And I don't want you all going against me on this. I want to give her the benefit of the doubt. I want to help her and Bax get past this trouble, whatever it is."

The men looked at each other, then at Luke. Garrett said, "You're the one who knows her best, Luke. We trust your judgment. If you say she's all right, then she's all right. If you take her side, we've got your back."

"And if it turns out you were wrong," Wes said, "then we'll all be wrong with you."

Around him, the other men nodded in agreement. Luke lowered his head.

"Thanks. That means a lot."

"So? What have you found out? How can we help?"

The horse was dry now, and Wes opened the stall. Luke led her inside, and Elliot poured a scoop of grain for her. Garrett returned the other mount to its stall as well, and they all gathered in the middle of the stable in a semi-huddle.

"Baxter told me some men tried to shoot him and Jasmine, and he seems to think those men are still after them. Had a nightmare last night. Poor kid is terrified, and he's obviously been through something. Jasmine won't talk. But she's got two sets of ID in her purse. One belonging to Jenny Lee Walker and one to Jasmine Delaney Jones. And the photo on the Jenny Lee Walker license looks nothing like Jasmine. It's not the same woman."

"So Jasmine *isn't* a nickname. And she's not this Jenny Lee she claims to be," Adam said slowly. "So that means she has no real claim to your place."

"Right. And even if she did, I don't think she ever meant to stay long. She admitted as much. Said she just needed a safe place to figure things out. And she keeps insisting she and Baxter are gonna have to move on soon."

"Probably figures whoever's after her will catch up," Adam continued.

"Shoot, better they catch up to her here than anywhere else," Elliot said. "We can handle them if they show up here."

"That's what I've been trying to tell Jasmine," Luke said. "She's not buying it."

"What else?" Garrett asked. "There's obviously something else. What is it, Luke?"

Luke swallowed hard. "She's carrying a gun."

Garrett lowered his head, swore under his breath.

"I found it in her bag. A little .32 caliber revolver. Unloaded, and I didn't find any bullets. She must have them stashed somewhere else."

"At least she's using sense about it," Garrett said. He shook his head. "Look, I'm going into the office. I'll boot up the computers and see what I can find out on her, under either name. I can at least check wants and warrants."

"Garrett, I told you, she's not the one who's broken the law here," Luke said, instantly defensive. "I'm sure of that! All she's done is try to protect herself and her boy."

"Hey, take it easy. I believe you." Garrett's tone, his expression, were sincere. "But that doesn't mean she might not be in legal trouble. Innocent or otherwise. Or she might be wanted for questioning, as a material witness to something else. I have to check. It's just a starting point. If her name—either of her names—comes up anywhere, it gives us a place to begin trying to figure out how to help her."

"And how to protect her," Lash put in. "Chicago's a rough town. Don't forget, I'm from there. And I still know folks there—that might be helpful in this."

Drawing a breath, Luke sighed. "Okay. All right, fine. But I'm coming with you, Garrett. I want to know what you find out."

"It's gonna be all right," Garrett assured him. "Lash, you'd best come along with us, too. Wes, Ben, Adam and Elliot, you get on out to the water hole and keep an eye on things. Don't let Jasmine or Baxter out of your sight until we get back, okay?"

They nodded and headed out. Garrett closed the stable doors behind himself, Luke and Lash, and the three of them piled into his pickup truck.

But what came up on the computer in Garrett's office in town was more than Luke wished he had seen.

"I really don't get it," Jasmine said. "I could have driven Bax and me home all by myself. I mean, it isn't like Luke would have been upset or anything."

"Oh, no, he wouldn't have cared in the least." Wes wheeled Luke's pickup into the driveway of the once-stately redbrick house and braked to a stop. Jasmine was crammed between him and his oversize brother Ben. Baxter was comfy on Ben's lap, apparently enjoying the ride.

"Then why did you two insist on coming with us?" Jasmine asked, looking from the dark chiseled one to the big blond one.

"Because we didn't want you coming home all alone," Wes said.

"Yeah," Ben added, opening his door and climbing out with Bax still attached to him at the waist. "After all, it's different out here than it is in the city. Quiet and isolated, and we didn't want you two to feel nervous or scared or…you know, anything like that."

She slid her gaze to the big guy's. He had the sweetest blue eyes she'd ever seen, and she wondered for a second just what genetic miracle had resulted in a family of such damn fine-looking men. "Luke told you to keep an eye on us, didn't he?"

Wes looked at Ben, gave a shrug. "He did seem to think it would be a good idea if we hung around until he got back."

She lowered her head. She would have liked to think that Luke had set his two cousins on her heels because he didn't trust her. Because he thought she might run off with the silver or something. But she knew full well that wasn't the case. He had sent them to protect her, because he knew she was in danger. And he didn't even *have* any silver.

And while all her history and all her conditioning wanted to tell these two to take a hike, that she could damn well take care of herself, her experience since arriving on Luke Brand's doorstep told her something else. Because she felt safe, and watched over, in a way she never had. And she knew Baxter felt it, too.

She tipped her head to one side. "Bax likes hot cocoa before bed," she said. "You guys want to have some with us?"

The two men smiled and nodded. A weakness for sweets seemed to be another genetic component common to all the Brand men, she thought vaguely, and led the way inside. "Where did you say Luke went again?"

"Just to help Garrett with a few things in town. Probably loading up feed or something."

She lifted her brows, wondering what kind of small-town feed store would be open this late on a Sunday night, but she didn't ask. It was odd. Luke had slipped away once earlier in the day while she and Bax had been occupied at the big Brand family gathering. He'd taken his cousin Jessi with him. But hell, it was none of her business. She went to the kitchen to brew cocoa, while Ben and Wes sat in the living room with Baxter. She could hear them well. Ben was kindling a fire in the fireplace as the night grew cooler, and Wes was speaking to Baxter.

"Do you know I'm half-Indian?" he asked.

"You are?" Jasmine could hear the fascination in her son's voice.

"Mmm-hmm. Comanche."

"Wow," Baxter said. "Do you know how to shoot a bow and arrow?"

Wes's deep chuckle was so warm Jasmine knew he wasn't the kind to be offended by the innocent questions of a child. "I'm learning," he said. "But I do know other things. Do you know what a shaman is, Baxter?"

"No," Bax said softly.

"Sure you do," Ben said from the fireplace. "It's like a medicine man."

"Ooh, yeah. I've seen them in the movies. They shake rattles and dance and do magic and stuff."

"Exactly," Ben said. "Wes is a genuine Indian shaman. He knows all about Comanche magic and animal totems and all that kind of stuff."

Jasmine turned the cocoa down to let it simmer and slipped to the archway, intrigued, and eager to see if Wes were kidding or sincere.

He was sitting on the sofa, facing Baxter, and looking dead serious. And with the flames of Ben's fire leaping up beyond him, and the smell of the burning wood, Jasmine found herself believing every word.

"Do you really?" Baxter asked.

"Yes, I really do. And I've got some Comanche magic for you, right here." Wes bent his head, and removed a thong with a large stone pendent on the end from around his neck. He showed the greenish stone to Baxter. Jasmine thought it was little more than a tumbled gemstone, like you could find in any nature store for a buck or two.

"It's got a paw print on it," Baxter said.

"That's a wolf paw. And on the back..." He turned the stone over.

"Is that a wolf?" Bax breathed, eyes wide behind his glasses.

Wes nodded. "The spirit of the wolf is a friend of mine. My personal totem. And I've asked him to hang out with you for a while. He'll protect you from anything bad...nightmares or bad guys, or anything that comes along."

Baxter seemed speechless as Wes put the thong around his neck. He took the stone in his hands and stared at it, turning it over and over. "Is he real or pretend?"

"He's real. I met him once, in person. He came right up to me when I was camping out one night. I didn't know what to think. I thought he was just an ordinary wolf at first, and maybe I was gonna be his supper."

"Were you scared?"

"Oh, yeah, you bet I was. But he didn't bite me. He just stood there and stared at me, and I sat where I was and stared back at him. He's been with me ever since. See, he wasn't an ordinary wolf at all. He was the spirit of the wolf. And that's a whole different thing."

Baxter lowered his eyes. "Then he's not real?"

Poking another log onto the burgeoning fire, Ben laughed. "That's what I used to think about all Wes's mumbo jumbo, kid. But I've seen enough to know better by now."

"He's real," Wes said. "He'll come around if he's needed. Until then, he kind of hangs out in the shadows, just keeping an eye on things. You don't see him, but that doesn't mean he's not there. Now, it's not that I think you need extra protection, because you're probably the safest little guy in Texas, with Luke and your mom right here, and the rest of us just down the road a piece. But I heard you had a nightmare, so I thought this might help you feel even safer."

Releasing the stone and letting it hang against his chest, Baxter said, "Thanks, Mr. Brand."

"You call me Uncle Wes, just like Bubba does, okay, Bax?"

Baxter smiled. "Okay."

Then Wes shook his hand, as if Baxter were an adult instead of a little boy. And Jasmine could see the way he sat up straighter in response to that.

She backed away as they continued talking. She poured the cocoa into mugs and carried them into the living room. The men sipped, and Baxter gulped. Then her son surprised her by saying he was going up to bed all by himself. He didn't seem the least bit afraid.

Ben volunteered to tuck him in and tell him a story, though, and Bax didn't argue. When they were alone, she looked at Wes. "That was a special thing you did, giving him that stone. Thank you."

He held up a hand as if fending off her thanks. "He's a special kid. I just wish it was as easy to convince grown-ups that they're safe and protected.''

She averted her eyes.

"Now, I don't want to butt in, Jasmine. But I like you. My whole family likes you, and Luke...well, Luke needs to speak for himself, I guess. But we all know for a fact that no matter what it is that's chased you all the way from Chicago, it can't hurt you here.''

She sighed softly. "I only wish that were true.''

Wes seemed to study her for a moment. Then he went on. "Do you think you showed up here by accident?''

Jasmine tilted her head to one side. "What do you mean?''

Wes shrugged. "That packet of legal papers that led you here—I don't believe it just happened to show up at the exact moment when you needed a haven. You were led here, Jasmine, because there is nowhere else in the world where you and Baxter could be as safe as you are right here.''

She narrowed her eyes on him, tilting her head to one side. "You really believe that?''

"I know it. We can help you. But only if you work up the courage to stop running. To turn and face it, and to stand and fight it, whatever it is. There's never gonna be a better time.''

She swallowed hard. She could almost believe him. But damn, she barely knew these people, this family. How could she put them at risk with her troubles? How could she put her son's life in their hands? How, when everything in her was screaming at her to take Baxter and run, and to keep on running?

A vehicle pulled in, and Jasmine tensed. Wes went to the window and looked out. "It's okay. Just Garrett dropping Luke off."

She took a breath, then got to her feet as she heard Ben clomping down the stairs. "Sounds like our ride home."

Jasmine nodded. "Thanks, you two. You really did take it above and beyond tonight."

Ben, much to her surprise, walked right up to her and gave her a hug. His big arms closed around her and squeezed. She tensed automatically, even now expecting a grope, a pinch, a bit of hip action. Something. There wasn't any. It was the kind of hug a brother would give to a sister. And there wasn't even a hint of anything else to it. He let her go and looked down at her. "We really, really hope you decide to stay, Jasmine. Penny and I want you to work with us at the dojo, teach those dance classes. And Bax is already like one of the family. You think about it, okay?"

For some reason she couldn't have hoped to name, her eyes were burning. She blinked, and muttered a response in a tight voice. Ben ruffled her hair the way he'd done to Baxter on occasion, and he and Wes turned to leave. When Jasmine turned to watch them go, she saw that Luke was standing in the doorway.

The men said their goodbyes. She heard Wes tell Luke to put him on speed-dial and call at the first sign of trouble. Luke nodded. But his face was drawn and tight when he came in.

At first she thought it was because of what he'd seen. Ben hugging her the way he did. "That wasn't anything inappropriate, you know," she said. "I've been groped by enough men to know when someone's up to no good, and your cousin wasn't."

Luke blinked out of his distracted state and closed the door behind him as he came inside. "I know," he said.

She blinked, frowned. "You know? How do you know? You trust him that much?"

He smiled. "Yes. But even if I didn't, there's the fact that Ben would burn out his own eyes before he'd look at another woman. He's completely devoted to Penny."

She pursed her lips. "Seems to be another Brand trait."

"The one-woman-man bit?" he asked. "Yeah, it does, doesn't it? I don't know how the hell it missed my father."

Jasmine tilted her head to one side. "He cheated on your mother?"

"He never married my mother. He did marry two other women, though, both at the same time. Fathered kids by all three. And who the hell knows how many more?''

She shrugged. ''And his brother was the father of all those cousins of yours?'' she asked.

''Yeah. Maybe it skips a generation. Orrin cheated on his wife, too. Only once, but still, Wes is the result.''

''Oh. I wondered about that.''

He looked at her, and she thought he looked tired. Bags under his eyes, a weary look to his drawn mouth. ''Is Bax asleep?''

''Yeah. You want some cocoa or anything?''

He shook his head slowly from side to side. ''No, Jasmine. All I want is the truth. We need to talk.''

She met his eyes, swallowed hard and backed up a step. ''Where did you really go with your cousin the sheriff tonight?'' she asked him.

''To his office. To run your name—or should I say your names?—through the computer.''

She blinked rapidly. ''And what did you find?''

''I found that Jenny Lee Walker was murdered, and that there's a warrant out for your arrest for the crime. They're saying you killed her, Jasmine. And I know you have her wallet. Her credit cards. Her license. Her legal documents. And a gun in your bag. So now I want you to tell me what the hell is going on.''

She turned her back on him. ''How long before your cousin comes back to arrest me?'' she asked.

* * *

Luke could see in her eyes that she was going to run. The way she backed away so he couldn't touch her if he wanted to. The way she kept glancing past him toward the front door, and then over her shoulder toward the stairs. She was calculating how she could race up there, grab her son and flee into the night without letting him stop her. Her eyes were so wide and so damned pained that he ached just looking at her.

He didn't move toward her, because he was sure she would run like hell if he did. Instead, he held up both hands, palms facing her. "No one's going to arrest you. Garrett punched all the buttons and then left the room before anything came up on the screen. He didn't want to be put in a position of having to choose between upholding the law and keeping his word to me."

She rolled her eyes. "As if there would be any question of which he'd choose."

"You're right, there wouldn't have been. He'd choose breaking the law so he could keep his word to me. Risking his job, losing it most likely. It wouldn't even have been a contest. But since he prefers not to lose his job over this, he figured he'd turn his back. I think the political types call it plausible deniability."

She narrowed her eyes on him, doubting him, he knew.

"Look, Garrett was just here, wasn't he? If he were going to arrest you, he'd have done it. He trusts my judgment, and I don't think you're a killer. I'm willing to look the other way on the warrant until we figure this out. And Garrett...well, as far as he knows for sure, Jenny Lee Walker is alive and well and standing here in my living room.''

She blinked. He thought her stance eased just a little. She breathed, but it was a broken, stuttering breath. ''Why do you believe in me, Luke? You don't know anything about me except that I'm an unwed mother, a former stripper, a liar, a total screwup....'' Her body was shaking now, too, in time with her breaths, and her eyes were brimming.

He moved closer, slowly, put his hands on her shoulders. ''You wanna know what I know about you? Hmm?''

She lifted her wet eyes to his.

''You're the most devoted mother I've ever seen. You'd step in front of a speeding truck for Baxter, if it came to that. And I think maybe you have, a time or two. You're an incredibly talented dancer. You move like the wind, and watching you makes me get all choked up somehow. You're terrified, scared right to death of something right now, and you're afraid to trust me—probably because I'm a man and you've never yet met a man who did you anything but wrong. And everything you've done— no matter what it might have been or how bad it might seem—you did to protect Baxter. And that includes lying to me about who you are.''

She lowered her head. ''You don't need the kind

of trouble I'm in, Luke. You don't want it, trust me.''

He hooked a finger under her chin. Then he leaned down and pressed his mouth to hers. He tasted the same sweetness he'd tasted on her lips before. A little gloss, a little color, a little cocoa and the salt of her tears this time, too. But he tasted more of her this time, because she let him. She didn't go stiff, and she didn't pull away. She stood still and let him explore her mouth, and she moved hers beneath it. He didn't embrace her, he just kissed her. She didn't fall against his chest. She just stood there, trembling.

And finally he lifted his head away. He said, ''I need to be completely honest with you, Jasmine. I'm scared. I'm scared to death of wanting you as much as I do—because it isn't like any kind of one-night-stand wanting I've ever felt before. It's something more. My father was a bastard who could no more stay with one woman than fly to the moon. He was no kind of father to me at all, and I grew up my whole life with my mother telling me I was just like him. For a long time I believed it. Until I came out here, found this bunch of cowboys who turned out to be family, and saw that I wasn't just my father's blood. I was theirs, as well. And maybe I could be the kind of man my father never was. And maybe I could have the kind of life I never had. A solid home. A real family.

''But that's just a maybe. I don't know for sure.

I don't know if I can be what I plainly see you and Baxter need more than you need air. I don't know.''

She frowned at him. "I didn't ask—"

"I do know that I can help you. Me and my family, we can help you get through this mess. And I know that I want you to stay and let us do that. After that...hell, Jasmine, we're just gonna have to wait and see."

She stared at him as if he'd grown a second head. "What did I ever say or do to make you think I was expecting you to take care of me or to become some kind of father figure to Baxter? Huh? Did I once suggest that I wanted to be some kind of small-town farm wife? Do I *look* to you like I belong out here in the middle of nowhere, chasing chickens with a broom? Do I? And as far as my sharing my son with you—with anyone—"

He was stunned. "I didn't mean...I was only trying..."

"You are so full of yourself, you know that? You are so freaking full of yourself. What, do you think I'm whiling away my hours fantasizing about you marrying me or something? You're insane!"

"Look, I insulted you, and I hurt you, and that wasn't what I meant to do. I was just trying to explain why I'm not on my knees groveling at your feet like any sane, rational man would be doing by now."

"It wouldn't matter if you were, Luke Brand. I grew up with a mother who cared more about whatever low-life man she was sleeping with at the moment than about her only child. I grew up waking to no breakfast, to empty bottles and overflowing ashtrays, and my mother hungover in bed with a stranger. I grew up to her brushing me off, sending me to my room, shooing me away so she could have her fun, and I vowed—I *vowed*—that I would never let any man come between my baby and me. He is the only person I need in my life. And I love him so much that I don't have any love left over to give to anyone else. So you can just take your stupid ideas and—"

"I'm sorry. Jasmine, please, I'm sorry. I did this wrong, and you're upset anyway, and this is way too soon for any of this, and we got way off the subject."

She sniffed and kept her face averted. He thought maybe some of those tears had spilled over, but she wouldn't let him see, and he didn't want to force it. "You're right, we did get off the subject, didn't we? You wanted me to tell you whether or not I murdered my best friend in the entire universe. The answer is no. I didn't kill Rosebud."

"Rosebud? Jenny Lee Walker was Rosebud?"

She rushed right on, not hearing him or not wanting to. "I'm just as guilty as if I did, though. It's my fault she's dead. The man who killed her was looking for me. She got in the way. Now, will you just leave me the hell alone?" She started for the stairs.

He said, "No."

She stopped, went stiff, but didn't face him. "What?"

"I said no. I'm not gonna leave you alone. You've been alone way too long already. You can be as mad at me as you want to, Jasmine, but I'm not gonna leave you alone, and my family's not gonna leave you alone. We're gonna be here, all of us, from now on. And I'll tell you right now, if you go running off in the dead of night, I'm coming after you. I'm gonna make things okay for you and Baxter again somehow. But I'm definitely not gonna leave you alone. Not for a minute."

Chapter 10

The bedroom right next to Baxter's had a light on, glowing warm through the open door. She peeked inside when she passed and saw that the bed was all made up with a pretty comforter and fluffy pillows. There was a vase full of flowers, and a small clock on the bedside stand. She stood there for a minute, just looking. When had anyone had the time to...and who would bother...? Was this supposed to be for her? There was a small frame on that stand, too, with a snapshot inside. Glancing back down the stairs, she could only see Luke's back as he sat on the sofa, leaning on his knees and staring into the fire. Pensive. Silent. Lonely, she thought.

She turned back to the bedroom again, and this

time, stepped inside. An oval mirror that looked
like an antique hung on one wall. A small dresser
with four drawers, also very old looking, and with
a knob missing, was just beneath it, wearing a lace
dresser scarf. She moved closer to the little stand
beside the bed, bent to pick up the framed snapshot
for a closer look. It was Polaroid photo someone
must have taken just today—of Baxter sitting
proudly atop that pony of Bubba's. Her lips trembled, and Jasmine bit down to keep them still. Her
finger touched the glass over the photo, tracing the
brightest smile she'd ever seen her son wear as tears
welled in her eyes. God, he loved it here. He was
happier here than she had ever seen him. It had only
been a couple of days, and already he had better
color than he'd had before. His appetite was better.
He was spending more time outdoors than he ever
had, and loving every minute of it. Truth to tell, if
she could stay, raise her son here in this child-
friendly place, she would. But she couldn't. She just
couldn't, because Leo and Petronella would catch
up. She knew their kind. They were nothing like
the Brand men. They didn't have a shred of honor
or decency or care for anything besides themselves
and the thickness of their wallets. And they would
keep coming until they found her. The dream of
settling down in a nice town like this, of taking a
job giving dance classes for little girls, of raising
her son where he could be happy and secure, would
never be.

Unless...

She licked her lips as an idea formed in her mind. Maybe there was a way she could make those things happen. Maybe Wes Brand was right...that it was time for her to turn around and face the danger. To stand up and fight.

Luke sat up for hours, staring at the flames and wondering what he was feeling for Jasmine. If it was simple desire, then why did it twist him up in knots this way? And if it was more, then why was he so unsure? He'd undressed, tried to sleep, but the questions just wouldn't let him. What he felt for the boy, well, that was a different matter entirely. He loved the kid—almost fiercely. His heart swelled in his chest every time Bax looked up at him with those big intelligent eyes or shoved his glasses up on his nose with his forefinger. He wanted to fix everything that was wrong in the little guy's life and make sure nothing ever frightened him again. He wanted to watch those eyes light up when he brought home a puppy—or a pony. Or, hell, both. Why not?

He thought those feelings were a pretty good indication that he could stick with Baxter for the long haul. It was pretty obvious that he could never walk away from the kid, and it was even more obvious that it would rip Luke's heart out if Jasmine took Bax and walked away from *him*.

But what about Jasmine? What about her?

And as if thinking of her had conjured her somehow, he caught a whiff of her scent, so subtle it was barely there, but he never missed it when she was near. He heard the gentle brush of her feet on the stairs and sat up slowly, turning to look her way. It had been hours since she'd gone up to bed. And yet she didn't look as if she'd even undressed. She still wore the clothes she had earlier. Jeans that fit too good for a man's peace of mind, and a white button-down shirt that wouldn't have been sexy on anyone else.

"Can't sleep?" he asked her.

She swung her head toward him fast enough to let him know he'd startled her. "Uh, no. But I thought you'd have been out cold by now."

He shook his head. "Can't seem to shut my mind off."

Sighing, she shoved her hands in her jeans pockets and came toward him. "Bax and I have rained chaos down on your peaceful life out here, I guess."

"Hey, do I look like I mind?" He swung his legs off the couch, put his feet on the floor. Then, as her pretty eyes skimmed down him, he became acutely aware of his attire. A pair of boxers. Nothing else. Of course the blanket was still draped over his lap, but his knobby knees and hairy legs and bare feet were hers for the looking. Not to mention everything from the waist up. And she looked plenty. Then she looked at his face again, and she smiled.

"Are you blushing, Luke?"

He averted his gaze. "Just feeling a little exposed, is all." He tried to move the blanket to cover more of him.

"Hell, I've been seen by more eyes and in less clothes."

"Yeah, but I'll bet you looked a lot better." He was embarrassed right to his rapidly heating ears, and she, damn her, was coming closer. Her stockinged feet moved nearer, and she sat right down on the couch beside him.

She said, "Oh, I don't know. You aren't so bad, you know."

"No?" He managed to lift his head and meet her eyes. And he saw the teasing light in them.

"No. Well, except for those knobby knees."

He smiled with her. She had a way of putting him at ease, when she wanted to. "Knobby knees are one of the genetic traits the male members of the Brand clan try to keep secret."

"Guess I just found something to hold over you forever, then."

"Only if you plan to stick around that long."

Her smile died so suddenly that it was as if he'd slapped it away. And he was damned if he knew what insane urge had made him say the words he had. He must be losing his mind. But they were out there. There was no taking them back now.

Her voice very soft, she said, "The bedroom...is beautiful. Did you do that, Luke?"

"Yeah. Well, you know, I had some help from Chelsea and Jessi. We took turns slipping away during the day to add things. None of it's new or anything."

She said, "New or not, that's probably the nicest thing anyone's ever done for me."

He shrugged. "I just thought you ought to have some space of your own."

She nodded at the couch. "While you camp out on the sofa like a guest in your own home."

"There are lots more rooms upstairs. I'll fix one up for me when I get around to it."

She leaned back on his couch, pulled her legs up underneath her. "It's good here. Bax loves it here. And I think he's starting to love you, too."

"Don't think for a minute that it isn't mutual, Jasmine."

That made her smile. "You've done so much for us. You and your family. I can't believe I'm about to ask for even more." Her head lowered as she said the words, her hair falling like a curtain around her face.

He reached out, pushed her hair aside, gently tucking it behind her ear. "Don't be sorry. Especially not if you're finally gonna let me help you out of this mess you're in."

Lifting her head slowly, she smiled at him. "I didn't think they made men like you anymore. All ready to charge in and save the day. You're like something out of a story, you know that? But no,

Luke, what I'm asking of you is a hell of a lot more than that.''

''What, then?''

She drew a breath, a deep one, and lifted her chin. ''I want you to take care of my son if...if anything happens to me.''

Luke's brows came down hard. ''Honey, nothing's gonna happen to you. Hey, come on, is that why you've been awake all night? You've been lying up there thinking about...about...''

''About dying. Because that's what will happen if they find me—*when* they find me. And it's driving me insane worrying about what's going to happen to my son if I'm not here to take care of him anymore.''

He took both her shoulders and looked her firmly in the eye. ''You aren't going to die. For crying out loud, Jasmine, you can't be thinking like this.''

''Well, I am, and I will be until you tell me you'll take care of him.''

He searched her face, wondering how she could survive any of this with such a grim attitude. ''I can't believe there's any doubt in your mind that I would. Yes, Jasmine. I'd take care of Baxter if anything happened to you. I'd take care of him like he was my own. I promise you that. I'll swear it on the blood of every Brand who ever lived, if it'll make you feel better.''

''It wouldn't be easy, you know. They might still come after him.''

"I'm aware of that. Didn't you hear what I said? 'Like he was my own,' Jasmine."

Her lips trembled, and her eyes welled. Her breath seemed to stutter out of her, and she seemed to go limp as she sank against him. Luke put his arms around her, held her gently, felt her shoulders tremble beneath his hands. "Thank you," she whispered. "You can't know how much it means to me, what you just said. Thank you, Luke."

"Hell, Jasmine, don't cry. Please? You gotta stop thinking this way. Don't you know how safe you are here, with me? Hmm?"

She lifted her head from his chest and looked up at him.

"They'd have to go through me to get to you or Bax. And they'd better go through hard, because if there's a breath left in me, I'll spend it to keep you safe."

She blinked, as if shocked right to the core by his words. And he was damned if he knew where they were coming from. They just spewed out without warning or planning, or even bothering to ask his brain for consent.

She was stunned. Frankly, so was he. If a year ago someone had told him he would be saying things like this to woman, he would have laughed in their face.

He didn't know how to shut himself up, or how he could possibly finish those words. But then he didn't have to, because she was kissing him. Her mouth closed over his. She suckled his lips and licked his tongue, and tears were streaming down her face the whole time. He kissed her back, just as eagerly. He held her hard, while her hands pushed his blanket away as if it were some unbearable annoyance. His hand cupped the back of her head, his fingers buried in her hair as he held her to him and tasted her, exploring her mouth the way he'd been wanting to do. This was what he'd dreamed of doing for hour after long, lonely hour. God, he didn't even know how badly he'd been wanting her until now. He was on fire just from this kiss.

She pushed him backward on the couch, and she bent over him, dragging her warm mouth away from his, and over his neck, to his chest. She used her tongue, even her teeth, to make him squirm and ache and burn. Every part of him was trembling. Every inch of him alive and aware and in horrible fiery need.

Then suddenly she got up, her hand clasping his, she tugged him to his feet. He rose. His boxer shorts bearing a tent pole, he followed her. She said, "I don't want us to wake Bax," and she led him through the dining room and kitchen, and out the back door. He closed it behind him, following her as if he were in some kind of hypnotic trance. She walked a little ways from the house, her bare feet in the dew-wet grass. He shivered in the cold. Then she let go of his hand and moved away from him.

And then, under the stars, in the moonlight, she began to dance.

So sensual, the way she moved, that it took his breath away, and he thought he would explode from desire. When she slid her hands up her thighs over her hips and around to the button of her jeans, popped it free and slid the zipper down, Luke lost the feeling in his legs. He landed in the wet grass on his backside, and the shorts were wet, and he was shivering and burning up at the same time. She wriggled the jeans slowly, slowly down over her hips and her legs, but the shirt fell, too, covering the delectable tanned skin a split second after she revealed it to him. Teasing glimpses were all he was given of the curve of her hips and the tops of her thighs. The rest of her legs, though, were given to him fully and slowly. She kicked the jeans off, and he reached for her, but she danced just out of reach. She went to work on the panties next, again giving him fleeting glimpses as she worked them slowly down. Her rounded buttocks were revealed at inch at a time, no more. The little crease where backside met thigh. God, he wanted to kiss her there.

Finally her fingers nimbly released the buttons of the pristine white button-down shirt. One by one. Top to bottom. She turned her back to him and slid the shirt off her shoulders, lower and lower, revealing the curve of her back. Then she turned fast as she lowered it all the way and pulled the loose shirt around in front of her. A flash of her backside made his heart palpitate. And now she danced in front of him, holding that shirt over her beautiful body.

She danced closer to him, and closer still. He reached out, caught the edge of the shirt in one hand. She smiled at him, and he yanked it away. And then he looked his fill as she danced still more. He got to his feet, reached out and caught her waist in his hands. And then he pulled her tight to him, and he kissed her long and deeply. His hands could touch every part of her now, and they did. Her back, her buttocks, her thighs. He rubbed and caressed her as he probed her mouth with his tongue. Her hands tugged on his shorts until they dropped to the ground and he stepped out of them, kicked them aside.

Luke scooped Jasmine up off her feet and carried her to a spot beneath the wide branches of an oak tree, and then he laid her down and kissed her from her head to her toes and back again. He nursed at her breasts until she pulled his hair, and then he lingered there longer. She arched against his hand when he slid it toward her center, and so he touched her there, and then more deeply. The way she moved in his arms, beneath his touch, it seemed to Luke as if she were dancing still. And finally he lowered his body over hers and slid himself inside her.

She closed her eyes, and she whispered his name. She was incredible. The scent of her hair, of her body—he was completely surrounded in her, drowning in her, and relishing every bit of it.

Luke took his time. He made love to Jasmine more tenderly and more thoroughly than he'd ever made love before. He made her tremble all over, made her cry his name out loud, made her contort her beautiful face in anguished ecstasy. And then he held her tenderly, and he kissed her face.

And she said, "Thank you, Luke."

He lifted his brows, holding her closer, wishing for a blanket as the heat of passion slowly cooled and he felt the chill of night's kiss raising goose bumps on his skin. "The pleasure was all mine, lady."

"Not for that," she said with a little laugh. "For all you've done for Bax and me. And for the promise you made." She rolled toward him and gently brushed a hand through his hair. "I hope you realize now how much it's all meant to me. I don't do this sort of thing very often."

Luke lay very still, staring hard at her. "What?"

She smiled softly, rolled onto her back and sat up, rubbing her arms. "It's getting cold. Let's go inside." Looking around, she spotted her white shirt and bounced easily to her feet to pick it up, pull it on.

"In a minute," he said. "First…tell me what you meant by that."

"By what?" She was fastening buttons now. One, then the next.

"By what you just said. That you were grateful to me—Jasmine, is that what this was all about? You showing gratitude? You thanking me for something?"

"Only partly." She blinked and stared at him. "I wouldn't have made love to you just out of gratitude," she told him, coming closer. "I wanted you. You wanted me. I like you. You like me. And I owed you...something special. Something as special as what you've done for me and Bax." She shrugged. "It just...felt like the right thing to do."

Luke lowered his head. He drew a breath, but for some reason his chest hurt. His throat was tight. He'd thought...he'd thought...hell, he didn't even want to think about what he'd thought. He was an idiot.

"Luke?" She was right in front of him, now, wearing that shirt and nothing else, one hand on his cheek. "Are you mad at me?"

"Of course I'm not mad at you."

"Then what's wrong?"

He lifted his head and looked into her deep, wary eyes. She was like a wild thing. So untrusting, so afraid. Sex didn't mean love, because sex was a commodity and love was a weakness. She'd repaid him with sex. But she wasn't going to risk her heart on anything more.

And how could he blame her when, up until five minutes ago, he'd been more or less oblivious to his own feelings?

My God, he loved her. But if he said so, she would run like a doe from the archer. He licked his lips. "Nothing's wrong, Jasmine. Just...next time you think you owe me something, tell me first, okay?"

"You telling me you didn't like my method of payback?" She slid her hands up his chest and pressed a kiss to his mouth.

"Oh, I liked it fine," he whispered. Then he caught hold of himself, cleared his throat. "But I'd have liked it better if it had been for other reasons."

She frowned and stepped away from him. "I never knew a man to give a damn about the motivations behind a woman offering him sex before, just so long as he got it."

"Yeah, well, you've been hanging around with the wrong kind of men, then."

She tilted her head to one side as if trying to puzzle him out. He shook his head, afraid he would say too much if he kept this conversation going. Instead, he slipped an arm around her shoulders and headed her toward the house, bending to scoop up discarded clothes along the way. "Don't ever feel you have to repay me in any way for anything I do, okay, Jasmine?" he asked softly. "If I do something, it's because I want to do it. You don't owe me anything."

She leaned her head on his shoulder. "I don't understand you."

"No," he said. "I don't suppose you do."

They went inside, where she kissed him good-night and headed up to her bedroom. Luke went to the sofa and pulled his covers over him. And though he was bothered by her motivations, he didn't dwell on it long. His body was satisfied, and his soul drained. He was asleep moments after his head hit the pillow.

When Luke woke, the sun was streaming in through the eastern windows, the fire was long dead, and he was no closer to knowing all the answers. He only knew that he had somehow managed to fall in love with a woman who didn't seem to believe love existed. But he knew it did. Now, for the first time he could recall, he really knew it did.

Maybe he should tell her. No, no, maybe he should see to first things first here and stop thinking like a teenager with his first crush. Maybe he should take care of business—namely, eliminating the threat to Jasmine and her son. That had to come before anything else. How could he expect Jasmine to think about tender emotions and lifetime commitments when she had this threat hanging over her head?

That was it. That was exactly it. He had to go to Chicago. Simple. He didn't know why the hell he hadn't thought of it sooner. He was the man here. He was a Brand, for heaven's sake. He didn't need to wait for Jasmine's permission to get involved.

He needed to take this bull by the horns and twist until he broke its damned neck. Period.

He got up and ran upstairs, animated now that he had chosen a course of action, eager to get on with it. He tapped only once before opening the door to the bedroom he'd fixed up for Jasmine, with loads of help from his cousins-in-law. But she wasn't there, and the pretty comforter was undisturbed. The bed hadn't been slept in. Maybe she'd decided to sleep with her son. God, he hoped Bax hadn't had another bad dream. Luke had slept like a log last night—he could have slept right through it. He stepped into the hallway and turned to Baxter's room. But when he opened that door, he didn't like what he saw there at all. Bax, huddled on the bed with his knees drawn up to his chest, crying as if his little heart were broken in two. His glasses lay on the bed beside him, as if he'd had them on, but taken them off again.

Luke's own heart split open at the sight of the tears on the boy's face, and he quickly went to Bax, wrapped him in his arms and held him close. "Hey, now, come on. What's all this?" Bax hugged him back but didn't speak. If anything, his sobs got louder. "Baxter, come on, pal, tell me what's wrong. Did you have another nightmare? Hmm? Is that it?" The small head shook side to side very slightly, all without moving from Luke's shoulder. "No? Well, what then? Hmm? Come, on, Bax, you know whatever it is, I can make it better. You know that, right?''

Silence. The crying stopped, though a few spasmodic sobs kept on coming, like aftershocks, quaking Baxter's small body. He lifted his head, and he looked Luke right in the eyes, even though his were slightly unfocused without his glasses. ''You can? You really, really can make it better, Luke? You're not just saying that?''

''I'm not just saying that. Whatever is wrong right now, I promise you, I will fix it. I'll find a way. But I can't until you tell me what it is.'' He wanted to ask where Jasmine was. In the bathroom, maybe. He didn't hear the shower running, but that didn't mean much. But he would get to that later. First things first here.

Swiping his wet cheeks with the sleeves of his pajamas, Baxter lifted a hand and opened it to reveal a crumpled sheet of paper. Frowning, Luke took it and slowly smoothed it open. And then he read the lines with a sinking heart.

My sweet little boy,
Mommy has to go away for just a little while. But I know you will be safe and sound here with Luke and the Brands. They'll take very good care of you until I get back, and I promise that won't be very long. You are the most precious thing in all the world to me, and I could never stay away from you for very long.

You know that. Please don't be worried.
Mommy's gonna make everything all right
again. You be a good boy. I'll be with you
again soon.
Love, Mommy

Chapter 11

Luke closed his eyes slowly, trying to digest what he was reading. But they popped open again when Baxter said, "She's gone back to Chicago. I know she has. She's going to try to get those men so they can't get me. Luke, they'll hurt her. I know they will! You have to do something."

Luke cupped the boy's face and said, "You bet I'll do something. Come on now, son. You need to get up and dressed. And you need to tell me everything that happened before you and your mom left Chicago, so that I can go fetch her back here safe and sound, all right?"

Baxter nodded.

"I won't let anything happen to her, Bax. I promise."

Baxter looked up into Luke's eyes, searching them, looking for something. Then, finally, he nodded. "Okay," he said. "I believe you."

Twenty minutes later, Baxter and Luke stood on the porch of the ranch house at the Texas Brand, and Luke thumped on the door twice. It was Bubba who pulled the door open, and he grinned ear to ear when he saw Baxter standing there. "Hey! I was gonna call you anyway this morning!" Bubba said.

"Why's that?" Baxter asked.

"'Cause I'm gonna go fishing in the water hole, and I was gonna ask you to come along. You want to?"

Baxter turned to look up at Luke, big eyes questioning. Luke hunkered down, clasped the boy's shoulders. "I gave you my word, Bax. I don't ever go back on my word. I'll bring her home safe. You don't need to worry. You just have fun with Bubba and try not to think about anything other than the fact that your mom will be with you very, very soon. And all this trouble will be history. Okay?"

Bax nodded his head.

"You want to go fishing with Bubba?"

Again he nodded.

"Then you go ahead. Next time you see me, I'll have your mom with me. Okay?"

"Okay." Bax leaned in and hugged Luke's neck. "Don't take too long, Luke."

"I'll be as fast as I can, son."

When Bax let go, Bubba grabbed his hand. "Come on, I'll show you my new fishin' pole. I've got three now. Tell you what, you can use whichever one you want." He was still chattering as he led Bax outside and toward the shed beside the stable.

Luke watched the boys go, turning only when Garrett spoke. "So what happened?"

Luke faced him, saw Chelsea at his side, worry in her eyes. "She's gone. She left a note for Bax saying she was gonna make things right for him, and she'd be back soon."

Chelsea closed her eyes slowly. "She went after whoever's been dogging her."

"What the hell is it with you women, anyway?" Garrett muttered.

"She's protecting her son, Garrett. A mother would face down armies to protect her child," Chelsea said.

Luke sighed. "Look, if you'll just keep Baxter for me, I'll head up there and take care of this. But I have to hurry. I don't know how much of a start she has and—"

"Hold on, hold on," Garrett said, holding up both hands. "Luke, I know you're new to the clan here, but that's just not the way we do things."

Luke tensed. He lifted his chin. "I'm going after her, Garrett. There's nothing you can do to stop me, or to talk me out of it, and I don't have time to stand here while you try. She's in trouble, and I'm going after her.''

Garrett nodded impatiently. ''Yeah, yeah, of course you're going after her. You just aren't going after her alone.'' He turned to Chelsea.

She said, ''I'll throw a few things in a bag for you. You'd better call the boys. Luke, don't worry, we'll have you guys on the road in twenty minutes—fifteen maybe.'' Then she hurried up the stairs, while Garrett went to the phone.

Within ten minutes, the driveway was lined with pickups and SUVs, and Brands were everywhere. It was the damnedest thing Luke had ever seen. Garrett had said nothing on the phone other than ''Jasmine's in trouble. We're going to Chicago. Pronto.'' And from what Luke could see, no one asked what, why, when or where. They just hung up and headed over here. They made minutemen look slow.

Lash and Adam were elected to stay home and keep tabs on the family and the Quinn Sheriff's Department—Lash being the only deputy. Ben, Garrett, Wes and Elliot all began stowing their gear in Ben's big SUV. It had the most room, so it was, by default, the vehicle they would take. There was no discussion on this, it just seemed they all knew it. And the stuff they tossed into the back made Luke wonder if they were used to preparing for all out war. There were shotguns, boxes of ammo, a rope, even a bullwhip, along with a small overnight backpack for each of them. It made Luke's duffel bag with a change of clothes and a toothbrush crammed inside look damned insignificant.

"They aren't going to let you bring those weapons into the city," Luke said, nodding at the guns.

"That's okay, cuz. We weren't planning to ask," Wes said, slamming Luke on the shoulder. "Did someone call Marcus?"

"He'll be here in an hour to help keep an eye on things here," Garrett said. "Bax will be well protected while we're gone." Then Garrett turned to Chelsea, and kissed her long and hard. "Don't worry, hon. I'll be back soon."

"I'll be waiting."

Bubba ran up and leaped into Garrett's arms, hugging his neck. "Be careful, Dad."

"Always. You take good care of Baxter, okay? I'm trusting you to see to it he doesn't have any skinned-up knees or broken bones when his mom gets back here."

Bubba grinned. "We'll take it easy. Promise."

"Good." Garrett put the boy down.

Luke saw Baxter standing beside him. He'd watched the entire exchange between father and son like a hungry pup eyeing a T-bone. Luke hunkered down and held out his arms. Baxter's face lit up, and he ran into them, hugging Luke's neck, and Luke's throat closed up almost too much to let his words through. How had the little guy wrapped himself up so tight in Luke's heart so fast? "Now, if you're gonna stay here, you'll have to help Bubba with his chores—you know, he has that pony to take care of. You're gonna have to help with that."

"Sure will, Luke." As Luke expected, Bax's eyes lit up at the prospect. Good. Poor fellow needed something on his mind besides his mother and the trouble she was heading into.

"And try not to worry. Everything's gonna be fine. I always keep my promises."

Nodding, Baxter released his neck. But then, impulsively, he grabbed on again and leaned in close, and whispered, "I wish you were my dad." He hugged hard then let Luke go, and, turning, ran back to the house with Bubba at his side. They stopped at the porch to pick up the fishing poles they'd left leaning there. Luke glanced toward Chelsea, but not right at her. He didn't think he'd ever been so close to shedding tears in his life—definitely not since he'd been Baxter's age himself. "You'll keep an eye on them around the water, won't you? I mean, I don't know if Bax can swim, and…"

Chelsea smiled wide. "Gee, you're starting to sound like Jasmine. Don't you worry, Luke. They aren't getting out of my sight."

He nodded, and finally turned and got into the SUV. He had to, because his eyes were burning more every time anyone opened their mouth. And what Baxter had whispered so desperately into his ear just now had hit him like a freight train. Because the response that had leaped to his lips was, "Me too." And he realized that he meant it.

Ben drove, since it was his vehicle, and Luke sat beside him in the front. In the middle set of seats with Wes, Garrett manned a cell phone, using his authority as sheriff to check with the airlines to be sure Jasmine hadn't booked a flight to Chicago. If she had, they would have to follow suit to catch up to her. When he finished speaking, he said, "No tickets bought to anywhere in Jasmine's name or Jenny Lee's. She has to be driving."

"That's good news," Elliot said. He was in the third row of seats, the one farthest back, his arms braced on the back of the seat in front of him, and his head leaning forward, between Garrett and Wes. "We might be able to catch her."

"She couldn't have left much before dawn," Luke told them. "I was...um...awake till then. And she had to walk past me to get out of the house."

"Why don't you fill us in on what you know, Luke?" Garrett asked. "I assume you at least have an idea of where to look once we hit Chicago."

Luke nodded. "Jasmine worked at a club called The Catwalk," he said. "Bax says they stopped on the way to take him to his last day of school so she could pick up her paycheck. She told him to stay in the car, but he got out, climbed up on some trash cans and looked in through a window. He says he saw three men in a room. One of them pulled out a gun and shot another one in the head."

Wes whistled long and low.

"Oh, it gets worse. Bax was so scared he fell, knocking the trash cans down. It made a hell of a racket, and he ran for all he was worth back to the car. The two guys came out the back door of the building, and Bax says one of them shot at him."

"Heartless bastard," Elliot muttered.

"You can say that again. Anyway, Jasmine came running, threw a brick at the shooter, and only managed to piss him off more. He turned the gun on her then, which I imagine, knowing Jasmine, was her intention all along."

Ben nodded. "Yep. To take the shooter's attention off Bax. Damn, she's a hell of a woman, Luke."

Luke nodded. "You'll get no argument from me on that score. At any rate, Bax put the car into gear and it shot forward. Jasmine jumped in, pushed Bax down on the floor and hightailed it out of there. Bax said they were going to go home, pick up Jasmine's roommate—another dancer who went by the name of Rosebud—and take off. Rosebud, by the way, was really Jenny Lee Walker. But when they got there, there were police cars outside, and they were carrying a body out of the building with a sheet over it. Bax said her hand fell free, and he saw it and knew it was Rosebud, and that she was dead. He also saw the cop who seemed to be in charge of things—and he swears it was the same guy who tried to kill him back at the club. He says his mother saw the man, too, and he thought that was why she was so scared.''

Garrett nodded slowly, taking it all in. ''Was Bax able to explain how Jasmine got hold of Rosebud's ID, and that packet from her lawyer?''

Luke nodded. ''He said Rosebud asked his mom to pick up her bag from the club while she was there picking up her check. Said Rosebud was forgetful—was always leaving her purse everywhere and having to go back for it. I'm assuming the envelope from the lawyer was there with it. The address on it was in care of The Catwalk, and I wondered about that from the first time I saw it.''

''So the question is,'' Wes said slowly, ''why the hell did they murder the roommate?''

''I've been wondering that myself,'' Luke said. ''But it's possible they didn't see Jasmine up close enough to know for sure who she was. If they looked around the place to see who'd been there, they'd have found both women's checks gone, and Rosebud's bag, as well. It could have been either one of them.''

''So they decided to just murder them both, to be safe?'' Elliot asked.

''And the little boy, too,'' Luke said. ''But when Jasmine and Bax got away, they decided to frame Jasmine for her best friend's murder. That's what I found in the computer last night. A warrant for her arrest. God knows it couldn't have taken much. Not when Rosebud's wallet, her latest paycheck, her credit cards and her roommate all turned up missing at once. They had to know they'd find those things on Jasmine when she finally turned up, making her look even more guilty.''

"Sure," Garrett said. "What better way to see to it they got their hands on her again than to put out a warrant on her? Especially on a murder charge. She'd be hunted down by law enforcement, brought back to Chicago as a prisoner and her son as a ward of the state. Easy prey at that point. For a man who calls himself a cop, anyway.''

Luke felt a darkness settle over his heart. "And now she's decided to face these animals all on her own. If they hurt her, I swear..."

Garrett's hand closed on his shoulder from behind. "We'll get there in time, Luke.''

"Yeah," Luke said softly. "Yeah. We have to.''

She drove for nearly twenty-four hours straight through, stopping briefly at an all night convenience store before she hit the club. She used the store's rest room mirror and most of the makeup in her bag, and she changed clothes. She needed to look like the same Jasmine who'd run away from here. But she didn't feel the same. Something...something had changed.

The club was dim when she arrived. Chairs upside down atop tables, nothing but ghosts inside. And Leo. He came out from the back, onto the main floor, never looking up to see her standing there, just inside the door, waiting. Jasmine had taken her time, made sure he was alone, before she'd come inside. Leo moved behind the bar, started wiping glasses and lining them up one by one. One of his early-morning rituals that always took place hours and hours before opening time. She'd known exactly where to find him.

Her high heels clicked with purpose as she stepped toward him, and Leo looked up from his task, spotting her at last. He looked as surprised as if he'd spotted Elvis coming toward him.

"Hello, Leo."

He smiled slyly. "Welcome back, Jasmine." He set down the glass he'd been polishing and slung the towel over his shoulder. "Where you been?"

"Around."

He shrugged, and one hand slipped out of sight beneath the counter. Jasmine brought her gun around in front of her. "Uh-uh-uh. Keep your palms flat to the bar, boss. Where I can see them."

Leo swallowed hard, his gaze focused on her gun, his Adam's apple bulging. "Just take it easy," he said. His palms slid flat to the bar's gleaming surface. "I know you're probably upset about Rosebud. Hell, we all are. You know, they think you did it."

"Lucky for me you know I didn't."

"Well sure I do! I never believed it for a minute, Jasmine. I tried to tell the cops that, but—"

"Come out from behind the bar," she snapped,

using the gun's barrel to direct him as he moved.
"Right here. Take a couple chairs down so we can
sit and have a talk." She reached behind her and
turned the dead bolt lock on the front door. She
knew the back one would be locked. It was almost
always locked. Only opened from the inside. She
stepped forward, waited for Leo to sit, and when he
did, she sat down opposite him. Out of his reach,
though.

"What do you want to talk about?"

"The dirty cop you're mixed up with, for start-
ers. The one who shot the undercover Fed in your
office last week. Petronella. What's his first name?
Gianni?"

Leo's brows slammed down hard. "So it *was* you
out there in the alley."

"It was me. You didn't see me?"

He shook his head. "Just the kid." Then he
looked up fast. "It wasn't me takin' shots at your
kid, Jasmine. It was him. I wouldn't hurt a kid. You
know that."

"I didn't see you trying to stop him."

"He'd have *popped me* if I had."

"Oh, hell, in that case, sure. Let him off a little
boy. Who wouldn't? Besides anyone with a soul."

Leo's eyes narrowed. "Is that gun even loaded?"

"You wanna find out?"

He went silent.

"So that's why you killed Rosebud. We shared
the car, and Bax was with her as often as with me.

You had no clue which one of us witnessed the murder.''

"I didn't have anything to do with…with what happened to Rosebud," Leo said.

"No?"

"No!"

"Then how did the bastard know where we lived?"

Leo lowered his head, averted his eyes. "Look, I don't like the guy any better than you do. But I don't have any choice but to deal with him."

"Why?"

He looked up slowly. "He's a cop. He could shut me down if he wanted to. You know damn well some of the girls take customers upstairs after a show."

"And you get a cut of the take."

"It's my bar."

Jasmine nodded. "And then there's the gambling."

"You know about that?"

She nodded once. "Every Saturday night in the back room, midnight till dawn. Sure I know about it. Everybody knows about it."

Sighing, Leo said, "Yeah, everybody. Including Gianni Petronella. When he found out about that, he upped the payment plan. Started demanding more and more of a payoff to look the other way, and even started showing up some weekends to play cards with the customers. And then this new kid came along. Terry Peck. Became a regular before we knew it. And he turned out to be a Fed."

"So you guys decided to kill him? Leo, do you have any idea how insane that is?"

"I didn't know Gianni was gonna pop the guy, I swear! He said we would meet with him in my office. Talk to him. When he pulled out that gun and put a bullet in him, I couldn't even believe it."

Nodding slowly, Jasmine said, "Looks like you're in over your head, Leo. So am I. But I'll tell you what. We're gonna help each other out of it."

"Oh, no," Leo said. "I'm not making a move against Petronella. You think I wanna end up like that Fed? No way, I won't do it."

"Yes, you will, Leo. Because I've got sworn testimony sitting in a lawyer's office right now. I've written down everything I know, and I got friends to sign off on it, backing me up. If you don't do exactly what I tell you, it's going to the D.A. And you're going down. Not just for the gambling and the prostitution, Leo. But for killing a federal agent. I was there. I saw it. You understand?"

He shook his head. "I should've let him kill you."

"You didn't do a damn thing to stop him from killing me. My kid did that."

"Yeah, there you go, what about your kid? You make a move like this, Gianni Petronella will take his revenge out on him. You know that, don't you? The guy's ruthless.''

''My kid is in a place where a dozen guys like Gianni Petronella couldn't get at him. He's safe, Leo. But you aren't. Not unless you play this my way. We'll bring Petronella down. And we'll do it together. Or else. All right?''

Lowering his head, Leo swore a long streak. Then, finally, he lifted his head again, met her eyes and said, ''What do you want me to do?''

''First,'' she said, stiffening her resolve, calling up all her courage, ''I need my old job back.''

It was a long, tense drive, with stops only when absolutely necessary. They hit Chicago with little more than the name of the strip club and the directions Lash had written out for them. It took a road map and a telephone book to get more precise about locale, and a short while later, they were there. They parked next to the curb, in front of the brick building with the red door and a neon silhouette of a nude woman in the window over the words The Catwalk. The window was dark. There wasn't another vehicle in sight.

''I'll check out back,'' Wes said, getting out of the car. Without a word, Elliot got out and went with him. Luke nodded vaguely at them, and went to the front entrance. But it was locked, and he couldn't see much at all through the windowpane.

Behind him, Garrett said, ''We should have expected this, Luke. Places like this don't open till the sun goes down. Eight o'clock according to the sign there."

Luke grated his teeth to keep from shouting obscenities. Dammit, where was Jasmine? What the hell was she doing? She could be hurt...or worse, and he would never know.

"Back's deserted. No cars, no lights, the place is locked up tight," Elliot said as he and Ben came back around the corner

"We're just gonna have to wait it out, Luke," Ben told him gently.

"There has to be a way we can find her. Let's check the apartment where she used to live. The neighborhood. We can drive around." He stopped there, knowing how useless it would be. They would never find Jasmine in a place this big, not unless she wanted to be found. At least, not until she came back to the club. And Luke was certain she would.

Garrett herded them all back into the car. They spent the longest day of Luke's life chasing shadows, and they didn't find Jasmine. Of course they didn't. He'd known they wouldn't. And still it damn near killed him to stop hunting, even to go back to the club.

But things got considerably worse when, as they finally headed back to the club in order to be there when it opened, the SUV blew a tire.

* * *

The club was full to capacity when Jasmine took the stage—but it wasn't the way it had been before. Before, she and Rosebud used to dance, then scoop up the money thrown at them and laugh to themselves that men were so stupid. Now...hell, now she just felt disgusted by those men. Because she'd learned that it wasn't some kind of genetic fault of the male sex that made them act that way. All men weren't like the grunting hogs in the club. There were good men out there. Honest ones, who cared about more than glimpsing a strange woman's body or copping a feel or getting laid. There were men like Luke Brand.

She wouldn't have believed it possible a month ago. Now, though, her tolerance level for these other men had reached an all-time low. They made her physically ill. But she had put the plan into motion now, and she had to play it out. So she danced, and the bass pounded in her temples, and she smelled the booze, sweat and smoke of the place and wondered how she'd borne it for so long.

But then she saw what she wanted to see out there in the crowd. At his table, with Leo. Gianni Petronella. And one of the girls, a seasoned pro named Grace, was giving him a little lap dance, exactly as planned. Petronella was so distracted by the wriggling on his lap and the flesh in his face that he hadn't even noticed Jasmine yet. But when

Grace got up, he looked, and his face went cold.
Jasmine sent him a smile and saw his face tighten
with impotent rage. Because what could he do?
Blow her away right there on the stage? No, he
would have to wait. And then she would have him.

She finished her number and left the stage, leaving the bills scattered on the floor for the next
dancer to pick up. Backstage, she passed Grace.
"Did you get it?" she asked.

Grace nodded and slapped the cold metal into
Jasmine's hand. Jasmine glanced down at the clip
from Petronella's handgun. "Thanks, Grace," she
said.

"I loved Rosebud, too, you know," Grace told
her. "You get the bastard, hon."

Chapter 12

It was after ten when the five tired, hungry, cranky Brand men strode through the front doors of the inner-city strip club. Luke needed a shower, a shave and a change of clothes. Though to tell the truth, he didn't much care how he looked to patrons of a place like this one. Not that any of them were looking at him, anyway.

No. Their focus was elsewhere, and he couldn't much blame them.

A small red-tinted spotlight cut through the smoke-veiled room to fall on the woman who was just now slinking her way onto the stage in time with a pounding backbeat. She wore shoes that consisted of little more than a foot-long spike heel and a toe strap. Her long, shapely legs played a game of peek-a-boo from behind their weblike stockings. She wore long black gloves, a body suit made mostly of black mesh, with leg openings that seemed waist high, a strategically placed black feather boa and a sequined face mask. All told, not a hell of a lot. Men hooted and whistled and howled like wolves, and the music blasted louder, and the woman twined the boa around herself as if it was about to become her next lover. Hands reached and groped, and lewd remarks were shouted.

"Hey, baby, lean down here, I have what you need!"

"Jasmine," Luke whispered, tensing.

A hand came down on his shoulder. "Easy now," Garrett said.

The stage was only a small raised section of the floor, a platform about three feet higher than the rest of the room. The only thing between her curvaceous body gyrating on the stage and the groping, slavering drunks in the front row were a handful of sparsely placed bouncers.

One guy got between them and managed to plaster his palm to her backside before he got pushed back.

"Hold on now, Luke. Just take it easy!"

"I'll give them easy," Luke said, and he shook off Garrett's restraining hand and started shoving his way through bodies toward the stage.

"Ah, hell," Wes muttered. "It's gonna be that dive down in Pueblo Bonito all over again."

"Nah. We'll probably end up in an American jail this time," Elliot said, as he and the others began shoving their way through right behind Luke.

Luke paid little attention to whether or not they kept up. He plowed ahead until he reached the stage and, when a bouncer roughly the size and shape of a gorilla stepped up to block his path, he decked the guy. The bouncer went down hard. Luke used his chest as a step up to the stage. Someone yelled, and his masked beauty backed away as Luke strode up to her. Someone grabbed him from behind, and Luke spun around, swinging. His fist struck someone's jaw, and his attacker went down. But Luke wasn't the only one under attack at this point. In fact, the fight seemed to have spread from him to his cousins behind him, and even now was spreading further to uninvolved bystanders, who, upset at having their entertainment interrupted, were apparently amusing themselves by hauling off and popping the first guy who looked at them.

A chair flew past his head, and Luke grabbed his woman and pulled her low, out of its reach. Then he scooped her up, tossed her over his shoulder and strode across the stage, off the back of it and through the curtains there.

Petronella followed her into the back, just as Jasmine had intended. He came up behind her, gripped her arm and propelled her past the dressing room and into Leo's office. Good. That was exactly what she wanted.

"You don't need to manhandle me, Gianni," she told him. "I came back here to make a deal."

He closed the office door, threw the lock. "You got nothing I want," he said.

"How sure are you of that?" She walked to the desk, pulled out Leo's chair and sat down. "Look, if I were going to turn you in, don't you think I'd have done it by now? God knows I was mad enough to, after you murdered my roommate."

He narrowed his eyes. "You're coming with me," he said, pulling out his gun.

"And what if I don't? What are you gonna do? Shoot me right here, in a bar full of people?"

"Hell, sweetie, they won't even hear the shot with all the noise out front."

She frowned. It *was* noisier than hell out there.

"Come on. Let's keep this clean. Come on out to the car. I kill one more person in his office, Leo will have a heart attack."

She nodded slowly. "This isn't fair, you know. It wasn't my fault I walked into this damn bar when I did—just in time to see you put a bullet in that guy's head."

"Tough break," Petronella said. "But that's life."

"I heard he was some kind of cop," she asked.

"Fed. A damned nosy one."

She licked her lips. "So that's it. You have to kill me then?"

"I got no choice, babe. It's nothing personal."

Again she nodded. Then she glanced down at the telephone on Leo's desk. She said, "Did you get all that?"

Petronella frowned hard. "What? What are you—"

"Every word," a voice said from the other end of the phone. "All of it on tape."

Petronella yanked out his gun, brandishing it at her. "What are you trying to pull?"

She shrugged. "Hell, Gianni, I'm just admiring the wonders of speaker phone. Leaves the hands free to run the tape recorder, you know? If you shoot me now, we'll have that murder on tape live, rather than just a confession."

Lunging forward, Petronella grabbed the phone's handset. "Who is this?" he demanded. "Where are you?"

But there was click and then a dial tone. Before he could think it through, Jasmine drummed her fingers over the keypad, hitting random numbers before Petronella yanked the phone off the desk and threw it on the floor. Now redial would do him no good, either.

"Whoever it was, they're on their way here with the police right now."

To her amazement, a distant siren punctuated the sentence.

Petronella backed away. "You think this is gonna save you? Do you? I'll find you, you smug little bitch. And your kid, too."

She shook her head. "Not if you're in jail, you won't."

He undid the lock, yanked open the door. A blast of sound rushed in, so much noise she thought a riot must have broken out in the bar. Petronella ran down the hall and out the back door. She stepped into the hall after him, but turned sharply at the sound of a familiar voice.

"That's it! I don't give a damn what your justification was, I don't want you dancing for men like that anymore. And maybe that sounds old-fashioned, and maybe you don't want any man telling you what to do." He was striding down the hall with a dancer flung over his shoulder. He stopped, set her down and softened his tone. "Well, fine, then, I won't tell you. I'm begging you. Please, don't get up on that stage again. It twists me all up inside."

The sounds of cracking bones and shattering glass came from the barroom. The sound of Petronella's car squealing away came from out back. Jasmine smiled crookedly, a little lump forming in her throat. The dancer wasn't so touched by Luke's emotional declaration, though. She hauled off and smacked him hard across the face.

Luke recoiled, blinking in shock. "What the hell was that for?"

"Maybe she doesn't like being manhandled by strangers," Jasmine said.

It was Jasmine's voice he heard, and it wasn't coming from the half-naked woman he'd just carried off the stage. He turned his head slowly and saw her standing there, looking less like the woman he'd fallen head over heels for and more like the one who'd first shown up on his doorstep. Big hair, coats of makeup, skimpy clothes.

"You've got to be kidding me," Elliot said from behind him. Luke turned to see Elliot, Garrett, Ben and Wes stumbling through the curtains into the backstage area off to the right. Each of them rubbing a different body part, they hurried to the hall. The riot out front seemed content to go on without them.

Luke swallowed hard and looked at the girl in front of him. Reaching out, he tugged off her face mask. She was cute and young and angry as hell. He shrugged. "Sorry."

Jasmine crossed her arms over her chest and glared at him. "So just what the hell do you think you're doing, Luke?"

"I...I thought she was you," he said in defense.

"Oh, and if she had been, that would have been all right? Dammit, Luke, I had a plan!"

"What, to dance around up there half-naked so the bad guys would be sure to have a good clear shot at you?"

The young dancer was looking from one of them to the other, wide-eyed, and backing away. "You're both crazy," she muttered.

"Yeah, well, you're too young to be stripping, so get your backside home before the sheriff here tosses you into jail," Luke muttered. He dragged his gaze away from Jasmine just long enough to send the girl a look that had her scurrying into the dressing room, slamming the door behind her, then he focused again on his reason for being here. His reason for being...period. He swore softly before he closed the distance between him and Jasmine in two long strides. Then he pulled her into his arms and hugged her hard to his chest. "Damn, I'm glad to see you alive."

She sighed in what sounded like exasperation. But she didn't pull away, and she even hugged him back. "Come on," she said. "Thanks to you, Petronella got away. But we have the goods on him now."

Luke backed off, glanced at her.

"I'll explain later. I just need to grab something out of Leo's office first."

She ducked back inside. Luke followed her, not knowing what the hell had transpired before he'd arrived. He watched as Jasmine went to a shelf in one corner, shoved some notebooks aside and pulled out a small camcorder. She pushed the stop button, then ejected a small tape. Then she went to the desk, opened the drawer and took out a mini-recorder, taking the microcassette from that, as well. Coming forward, she took his arm as sirens screamed outside.

"We'd better slip out the back," Jasmine said, leading Luke back into the hallway with his cousins. "Technically, I'm still wanted for murder."

"Wait up a sec," Elliot said. He tapped on the dressing room door. "Hey, come on, we'll give you a ride out of this hole."

"I'm not going anywhere with you lunatics," the dancer squeaked.

Elliot looked at Garret, brows raised. Garrett sighed. "Damn, I hate being the heavy. All right." He hauled his badge out of his pocket and walked into the dressing room. When he came out again, he had the girl by the arm. She looked scared half to death, but at least she was decently covered now in a long wrap, Luke saw with relief.

"Everyone, this is Misti," Jasmine said. "She's new here."

Luke pushed open the back door, and they all trooped out to Ben's SUV and piled in: Garrett in the front with Ben, Jasmine in the middle seat beside Luke, and in the back, Misti, Elliot and Wes. Police cars pulled up out front as they drove away. Their flashing red lights bathed the bar's open door and cast a strobe effect over the brawlers who'd spilled out into the street. Broken glass winked in the intermittent glow.

Jasmine shook her head. "What the hell did you guys *do* in there?"

"What, you don't know?" Elliot asked. "We *rescued* you!"

She rolled her eyes. "Leo will have to close down for a week just to fix the place up."

"That's gonna be a real drain on the moral fortitude of Chicago, I'll bet," Luke said.

She narrowed her eyes on him. "Some people depend on that place for their living."

"Yeah, well, some people depend on some pretty sleazy things in the name of money, Jasmine. That doesn't make them right."

"So now you're what, the Moral Majority?"

"Closest thing to it in this part of town."

"How dare you sit there and judge me?"

He blinked and stared at her. Somewhere, somehow, he'd gotten in over his head. "That's not what I was doing?"

"You damned well were!"

"No, I wasn't!"

"Were so," Misti put in with a huff. "And me, too."

"You don't need to be judged, you need to be grounded and sent to bed without supper."

"You wish," she snapped.

"I meant it literally, kid, not figuratively. And as for you," he said, and turned back to Jasmine.

"Stop this car and let me out," Jasmine said. "I've managed to get through my whole life without some half-baked male telling me how to run it. I don't intend to change now."

"Oh, and look where it's gotten you!" Luke said, his voice louder now.

Jasmine went utterly still, staring at him, stricken. "You mean the fact that I'm an unmarried mother who strips for a living?"

The pain in her voice, in her face, when she said those words to him shocked him into silence. He stammered, but nothing intelligible came out of his mouth, and then Jasmine opened her door and said, "Stop the car, Ben, or I'll jump out while it's moving."

Ben must have believed she meant it—Luke knew he sure as hell did—because he hit the brakes. Jasmine got out.

Garrett glared at Luke, and Wes shoved him. "Well, what are you waiting for? Go after her. We'll drive around the block till you've finished groveling, cuz."

Luke jumped out of the vehicle and took off after Jasmine. She moved fast for someone walking on five-inch railroad spikes, but he caught up in short order, gripped her shoulders and spun her around. "That's not what I meant, and you damned well know it," he managed to say. He'd been thinking up an appropriate apology for several yards and realized too late that wasn't it.

"Then just what *did* you mean? Hmm?" Hands

on her hips, she tapped one foot rapidly on the cracked sidewalk. "Well? I'm waiting?"

"I meant that making decisions on your own has gotten you into this situation that you're in right now. Running for your life, set up for murder, and too damned stubborn to let anyone help you."

"Oh, right. Like you?"

"Yeah. Like me."

"For your information, Luke, I had a plan back there. I gave Leo no choice but to cooperate, and it was working. I got Petronella admitting everything on tape. Audio *and* video! But you came along and distracted me, and he slipped away! I don't *need* your damned help!"

"I know you don't!" he shouted. Then, licking his lips, he lowered his head. "I know you don't. I came charging up here wanting to be your hero— like something out of a fairy tale, I guess. And here you were, doing just fine without me." He shrugged. "It's kind of deflating, you know?"

She seemed to soften just a little. "You...really? You came to rescue me? Like Elliot said?"

"Yeah. Really."

"Hey, mister," a voice said from behind him.

Luke waved a hand in the air without turning around to look. "Go away. I'm busy. Jasmine, I meant well, I really did. I was trying to save your life when I marched up on that stage the way I did."

She thought about that, then pouted, crossing her

arms over her chest. "No way, Luke. If you're going to be honest here, let's do it all the way. You were all ticked off 'cuz you thought that was me up there shaking my tassels in front of strangers. Admit it. You didn't give a single thought to my safety at that moment. You were just plain jealous and possessive, like some kind of bossy, overbearing Neanderthal."

"Mister!" the voice behind him said again.

"Dammit, can't you see I'm in the middle of something here?" Luke snapped. He turned partway around this time.

The kid stood behind him looking like yesterday's garbage. He had a blade in his hand, and he said, "Just gimme your wallet and you won't get hurt."

Jasmine sucked in a sharp breath. "Give it to him, Luke," she whispered.

"Oh, for crying out loud," Luke said. "Fine, here's my wallet." He punched the kid in the face so hard his nose crunched and his lip split. Blood spurted, and the kid went down. Luke bent long enough to snatch up the blade, whipped it over a nearby fence, then turned back to Jasmine again. "Look, maybe you're right, maybe I was out of line, and maybe it did bug me to see you—or think I saw you—dancing for all those men." He lowered his head. "If that makes me a closed-minded Neanderthal, then I guess I'm guilty."

She was staring at him, wide-eyed, her gaze darting every now and then to the kid on the ground behind him. Luke kept his eyes on Jasmine. He heard Ben's SUV coming around the block, recognized the sound of the engine.

"Come on, please? Just come with me. Someplace where we can talk? Please?"

Blinking slowly, she nodded. The SUV stopped, and they stepped around the kid, who was pulling himself to his feet. Luke held Jasmine's arm in one hand and opened the door for her with the other.

Garrett nodded toward the kid, who'd taken off at an uneven run, clutching his bloodied nose. "Trouble?"

Luke followed his gaze. "Not so you'd notice."

"Well, if Luke is done picking on the locals, can we get something to eat somewhere before we head back home? My belly button's touching my backbone," Elliot said.

Jasmine sighed, lowered her eyes. "I can't go back with you guys. Not until I finish what I came here to do."

She lifted her head again and met Luke's eyes. "And don't you dare try to tell me I can't. That man is still on the loose. He's still a threat to my son, and I'm not going anywhere until I see to it that he's not."

Luke set his jaw, deciding it was better not to reply to that just now. Drawing a calming breath, he said, "Get us back on the highway, Ben. Best truck stop in the state is ten miles out. We'll get a good meal there and figure out what we're doing next."

Very softly, a throat cleared. All eyes turned to Misti, whom Luke had forgotten was still with them. "What about me?" she asked.

"*You* are going back home to your family," Garrett said.

"No way," she snapped.

Garrett eyed her. "They abuse you?"

Her brows came down fast. "No. I just don't get along with my mom. She doesn't understand me." And she averted her eyes.

"Hell, kid, a few years ago she *was* you. Trust me on this. Now, tell me where you live so I don't have to haul you into some juvey center somewhere."

Pouting, clearly ticked off, but maybe just a tiny bit relieved, she said, "Cedar Lake, Indiana."

Elliot was already unfolding the map in the back seat.

Chapter 13

Two hours later, they sat in a big booth at a truck stop, three on each side of the Formica table. Jasmine had made a point to squeeze into the side with Garrett and Elliot, rather than on the other padded seat with Luke. He was crammed over there between Ben and Wes and looking as if he thought he was the wronged party here.

She really was doing her best to stay angry with him for chasing her up here, for telling her what to do, for leaving Baxter when he'd promised to take care of him. And mostly for acting so damned judgmental about her former career. Hell, it hurt that he thought badly of her. It hurt a hell of a lot more than it should.

And yet…she was touched in spite of herself that

he had come here after her, that he had wanted to be her hero.

They'd dropped Misti off at her house. Jasmine had tried like hell not to be affected by that little scene. A middle-aged woman in a housecoat had come to the door to see who was outside. When she saw Misti get out of the hulking vehicle, she burst into tears and ran down the steps, wrapping her up tight and thanking Jesus out loud. When Jasmine had looked around her, she'd seen the big, rugged Brand men at their dopiest. Every last one of them choked up and trying to hide it. She glimpsed ten damp eyes and five crooked smiles in that SUV. And as much as she knew about men, she realized she was only just beginning to know these men.

She watched them smile kindly at the harried waitress as they ordered enough food for an entire football team and told her to keep the coffee coming, and she knew they weren't flirting. They were genuine. It was freaking eerie.

Jasmine had never liked men. Baxter's father had worked hard to gain her trust. He'd conned her all the way into his bed, then vanished the day she told him she was pregnant. She'd been young and, she thought, in love. He'd broken her heart. She hadn't trusted men since, and she hadn't ever thought that would change. These men, however, had given her no choice in the matter. In spite of herself, she felt safe with them. She felt cared for. As if she were something important to them, something worth protecting.

Sighing, leaning back in her bench seat crammed between two of the creatures she'd spent her life detesting, she said, "So where's my son, Luke? You promised me you'd take care of him, and yet here you are, and I don't see him anywhere."

Luke met her eyes across the table. "Baxter was fine once he got done crying himself into fits over waking up to find his mother gone."

She flinched. That blow hit home. "I left so I could make things right for him."

"He knows that. You think that made it any easier?"

She lowered her eyes. "I didn't want to hurt him. It was the only way I could see to—"

"It was the only way you could see because you have tunnel vision." She lifted her head, ready to snap back at him, but he shook his head and went on. "He's staying with Chelsea and Bubba until we get back."

"And you think Chelsea and Bubba will be able to protect him if Gianni Petronella finds out where he is?"

"No. I don't. That's why Lash and Jessi are there, too, along with Adam and Kirsten, and Taylor and Penny and Esmeralda...the whole family is closing ranks around Baxter," Luke said. "And not just the local ones, either."

Frowning, Jasmine averted her eyes. But he went

right on. "By now I imagine Marcus and Casey have arrived, too—they only had a two-hour drive. Sara and Jake will make it in before the night's out. It's a longer haul from Gator's Bayou, Louisiana."

She lifted her head slowly. "I don't understand."

"That's because you've never had a family around you. That's the way family works, Jasmine. They pull together, they take care of each other."

She locked her gaze with his. "Baxter isn't part of your family. He's mine. I'm his family."

For a long, tense moment he stared back at her, and she knew her words had pissed him off on some level. Why, how, she wasn't sure. She didn't pretend to understand him, and she told herself she didn't want to try. But she knew that was a lie. Why, *why,* did she have to get so defensive where Bax was concerned? She knew Luke adored him.

"Shoot, don't try to tell Bubba that," Garrett said. His voice, lightened by his smile, broke the building tension. "He sure does think of Baxter as family."

"We all do," Wes said. "Family doesn't have to be bound by blood, Jasmine. Love is the real bond."

Ben nodded in agreement. "Rosebud was family to you, wasn't she?"

Jasmine closed her eyes slowly. "Rosebud was my best friend. She was like a sister to me, and she'd have given her right arm for Baxter."

"News flash, Jasmine," Elliot said from beside her. "So would any of us."

She shot Elliot a glance, but he was already looking away from her, focused now on the waitress who was bearing down on them with a laden tray. "Ahh, here comes sustenance. And not a moment too soon, either!" Elliot got up and took the tray from the woman's hands, then stood quietly while she lifted the plates of food from it and deposited them on the table. The whole time she worked, she wore this look of amazed gratitude. When the tray was empty and she took it from him again, Elliot said, "Thank you, ma'am," as he slid back into his seat.

She smiled. "Thank *me?* You keep this up, it'll be *me* leaving *you* a tip." Giving him a friendly wink, she strolled away.

Jasmine watched. Some guy at another table was glaring at the waitress and tapping his empty coffee cup, while another party waved impatiently to get her attention. The Brand men were different. No doubt about it. It got very quiet as they dug into their meals. Jasmine gnawed on her burger and fries without really tasting them, and wondered how in the hell she was going to find Gianni Petronella.

Luke didn't eat with as much gusto as the other men did, she noticed. He picked at his food, ate a little, but didn't seem to take much pleasure in it. Mostly he drank coffee. Lots of coffee. He met her eyes every now and then, looking as if he had something to say, but he never said it. Just looked away again until, finally, he excused himself.

Ten minutes later he was back, and he slapped two keys on the table, each with numbered plastic ovals attached. "I got us rooms for the night."

Jasmine wiped her mouth with a napkin and glanced at her watch.

"That bar will be closed for the night within an hour, Jasmine. Besides, Petronella won't go back there. You've been up for..." Luke looked at his watch. "Hell, *I've* been up for over forty hours. You, for longer. We need to get some rest, figure out our next step. Just stay here. You're safe with us, you know you are."

She lifted her brows, about to make some comment about how full of himself he was. But instead she recalled the punk on the street with the blade and the way Luke had reacted. She'd never seen anything like it. He was no more distracted by the kid than he would have been by a mosquito. Not even a little bit afraid. She did feel safe with him. And it was an odd sort of feeling. One she couldn't remember ever having before. It confused her on such a deep level that she couldn't even snap out a sarcastic reply. She just sat there, until finally she said, "So you're cramming us all into two rooms?"

He shook his head and dangled a third key from his hands. "Garrett and Ben get a room. Wes and Elliot get a room. You and I get a room."

Her brows came down hard, and her reaction was

automatic. "If you think for one minute that just because—"

"You've been under the same roof with me for long enough to know you can trust me, Jasmine. Twin beds, no ulterior motives except for the obvious one—I don't trust you not to run off the minute my back is turned. So I'm rooming with you. Period."

Jasmine got to her feet and poked him in the chest with a long, shiny fingernail. "No man tells me what to do. You room with your brothers. I'll room by myself." She snatched the key from his hand so fast he didn't have time to prevent it.

"Dammit, Jasmine—"

She strode out the diner's front door, underneath the jangling bells, and headed around to the rear, following the neon motel sign with the flickering arrow. She fully expected Luke would be right on her heels, and so she strode as purposefully as she could manage with her nose in the air and her heels clicking a no-nonsense cadence on the blacktop.

Three guys stood in a huddle, talking in the diesel-scented night air. Truckers, probably. Harmless, probably. But they looked at her as she passed, and she wondered what they thought they saw. Looking around, she saw where big rigs were parked in formation, an endless row of them. Here and there scantily clad women hopped up on the sides of them to rap on the doors and make their offers. "Need your truck cleaned, baby? Twenty bucks."

Jasmine's gaze slid back to the huddle of men. They were still eyeing her. Her short skirt and big hair and high heels probably made her look to them like one of the hookers who hung around places like this one. Then again, most of the patrons at The Catwalk made similar assumptions about her when she danced on that stage. They looked at her as if assessing a cut of meat, weighing its value against its price.

No one had looked at her that way in Quinn, Texas. Not even when she'd first arrived, in her short skirt and her high heels. Luke had never looked at her that way. Not even when she'd danced for him.

The men were coming closer now, smiling and speaking low to each other as they crossed the lot toward her. Where the hell was that pesky pain-in-the-ass cowboy, anyway? God, he followed her like a devoted hound when she didn't want him around, then vanished when she could actually use the help. He was *supposed* to follow her out of the diner. Damn him.

"Hey, honey," one said, but then he stopped walking, stopped talking, blinked twice and changed his attitude. "Um...I was just wondering which way to the rest rooms."

She frowned, wondering what the hell had changed his attitude. She glanced behind her but saw no one. Then she faced the men again, still some ten feet away from her. She lifted a hand, pointed the way, then continued her trek to the motel room. The men must have had a desperate need for that rest room because, when she glanced behind her to see where they were, they'd vanished. Long gone. Odd. Sighing, she searched for the door with the number that matched the one on the key she'd swiped from Luke, found it and let herself in.

Simple room. Twin beds, TV, bathroom, tacky framed prints on the walls with odd geometric patterns in primary colors. Jasmine closed the door behind her, turned the lock and sank onto the bed. It was late, after one in the morning, and she was tired. She'd driven a long way without sleep, and she'd come so close! Now she was just frustrated and cranky and exhausted. But she couldn't go to sleep. Not yet. She figured she would give the Brands an hour and then slip away. She would go to Leo's place and wake him, force him to tell her where this Gianni character lived, and then she would go to *his* house.

She reached into her handbag and touched the gun that was there. She'd taken the bullets out of hiding before she'd left the Brand place. The gun was loaded, and it was deadly. Gianni would either wait with her for the police to arrive and arrest him, or she would kill him. That simple. A shiver of unease worked up her spine when she thought of killing a man in cold blood. But then she thought about Rosebud, being shot down in her own apartment. She thought of that man turning and firing bullets at her own little boy. Shooting at a child with every intention of killing him. And when she thought about that, she really didn't think she would have any trouble at all pulling the trigger when the time came.

Besides, it was the only way. She needed him in prison or dead.

She took a cool shower to help wake herself up, and then she tugged more functional clothes out of the bottom of her deep bag. Jeans, flat shoes, a sleeveless denim button-down blouse. She scooped her heavy curls up into a ponytail, just to keep them out of the way. She didn't want her hair falling over her face or blocking her vision. She didn't want it providing a handhold for her enemy to latch on to, either. She'd thought about soaking off the long acrylic nails and decided against it. Pulling the trigger with them on would not be a problem. She'd tried it out on the way here. And the nails had the added benefit of being weapons in and of themselves. Every finger was as good as a small blade, with them in place.

Finally she was ready. She tucked the gun into the bag, stuffed the clothes she no longer wanted or needed into the trash—even the shoes. And went to the door of her room. Flicking the lock, she pulled the door open, looked both ways and stepped outside, only to trip over the big lump lying in front of the doorway. She nearly went headfirst onto the sidewalk, but the lump sat up and snagged her around the waist, pulling her down so she landed in his arms instead.

"Hey, Jasmine. Going out for a midnight stroll?" Luke asked, smiling innocently into her eyes.

She couldn't believe the nerve of the man! "What the hell are you doing camped outside my door?"

He shrugged. "You wouldn't let me share the room. It was the only way I could make sure you were safe."

"Safe from what!"

"From Leo, and this Gianni guy. I mean, suppose they followed us? Or got to Misti somehow and made her tell them where we were going? I don't plan to let them just walk in and shoot you the way they did your friend Rosebud, you know."

She started to speak, then stopped herself. There was a pillow behind him, and a blanket half over him. And she was on his lap, and his hands were anchored at her waist, and the way he looked at her was a way no one else had ever looked at her before. He looked at her eyes, then her lips, then her eyes again, over and over as he spoke. As if having trouble keeping focused. And her stomach did something funny, and instead of swearing at him, she heard herself say, "You've been sleeping out here on the sidewalk waiting for killers to show up?"

He said. "I wouldn't exactly call it sleeping."

She lowered her eyes.

"So where were you going, Jasmine?"

Inhaling deeply, she said, "To find Gianni."

"Yeah? And then what?"

Jasmine lifted her gaze to his. "Take him in or kill him, I guess."

"You do that, and even Garrett won't be able to keep you out of jail."

"Maybe not. But at least my son wouldn't have to be afraid anymore."

He stared into her eyes for a long time. "He'd be heartbroken instead. For the rest of his life, he'd hurt for the mother he lost."

She couldn't argue with that, so she didn't try. "At least he'd have a life."

"He has a life *now,* Jasmine. A good life. You made a fresh start in Texas. You have a good job waiting for you there, one you and Bax can both be proud of. You have friends there, people who care about you, and..." He let his voice trail off.

"And what?" she asked him. "And you? Are you going to say I have you? When we both know I'm the furthest thing from what you want. You told me yourself that you weren't ready for—"

"Dammit, Jasmine, will you just put the you and me part of this equation aside for a minute? I'm talking about you and Baxter and Quinn, Texas. I'm talking about you teaching dance at Ben's dojo. I'm talking about a place with enough fresh air and sunshine for Baxter to thrive on for years. Why do you want to turn the topic to you and me?''

She shrugged. ''You're the one camping on my doorstep and scooping me off stages and acting like you own me or something.''

He looked away. ''I didn't scoop you off any stage.''

''You thought it was me.''

''Hell, Jasmine, what do you want from me?''

She lifted her brows. ''I want you to walk away. Leave me alone. Just go back to Texas and forget all about me.'' She said it, but she knew that she was lying through her teeth.

He looked up at her slowly, held her gaze, and she was terrified for one brief moment that he would say ''All right'' and turn around and walk out of her life. She actually held her breath, and with every second that ticked by she expected him to say so long. But he didn't. Instead he said, ''I'm sorry, Jasmine, but I just can't do that.''

She almost sighed in relief. Did it show on her face? God, she hoped not. She hated feeling this way. No man had ever had her at this much of a disadvantage. If he knew, he would have the upper hand. She couldn't let on—dammit, she just couldn't.

So got herself upright, and she stepped back inside and held the door open, and said, ''I guess if you insist on being my shadow, you may as well come inside.''

He did, looking around, his eyes taking in every detail of the room, pausing on the wastebasket where the clothes she'd been wearing before draped over the edge and a single spiked heel stuck up like a potted plant. His lips pulled slightly at the corners, but other than that, there was no reaction, no comment.

He went casually to the bed on the left, flung back the covers and peeled off his jacket.

Jasmine managed to break the grip his eyes had on hers and turned away. "Don't you want to take a shower before you turn in?"

"And give you time to take off on me? No way. I'll wait till morning, thanks."

She shot him a glare. "And what's to stop me from taking off in the…"

He was peeling off his shirt now. Draping it over the back of a chair, then pausing, turning to catch her staring at him. She couldn't help it, though. He looked better undressed than she'd ever imagined a man could look. Firm and smooth and dark. Her palms heated and dampened as she remembered the way his skin felt beneath them—and then against hers. It had never been that way for her with any other man—so intense, so deep. Like it wasn't just her body performing the sex act. It was as if her whole being had been making love to him. And the memory of it just wouldn't stop haunting her. Teasing her. Even now.

She looked away quickly. "Never mind."

"What's to stop you from taking off in the morning?" he said, finishing her question for her. "My cousins, of course."

Fabric brushed skin, and a quick darting peek from the corner of her eye told her he was sliding those jeans off. She jerked her gaze away fast, tried to focus on the room straight ahead of her instead. But there was a damned mirror on the dresser, projecting his boxer shorts–clad body sliding into the bed, pulling up the covers, settling his head on the pillow. Then he lifted his head briefly, met her eyes in the mirror and sent her a wink. "Night, Jasmine."

She released a burst of noisy air, clenched her fists and stomped to her own bed. Damn him. Damn him! He knew how she was feeling, and he just wanted to torture her. To make her squirm. He didn't have to strip down to almost nothing. "This isn't fair," she snapped, yanking back the covers.

"What isn't?"

"You...showing up here and bossing me around. Keeping me from doing what I came here to do."

"Jasmine, for crying out loud, I came here to keep you from getting yourself killed. And to fix this thing once and for all."

"Oh, well, that's much better than my plan, which was to *get* killed and *not* fix this thing. Thank goodness you arrived!" She stood on the far side of the bed with her back to him, undid her jeans and slid them off, leaving the shirt in place. And

she couldn't help a quick glance at the mirror to
see where his eyes were. They were glued to her
legs, her thighs, and he looked like someone had
hit him in the belly with a mallet. Good.

She got into her bed, pulled her covers up over
her head, took off her shirt and bra, and then
emerged again, keeping the blankets chin high. She
flung the clothes toward the foot of the bed, where
they hung haphazardly.

He was staring at her with pained eyes. She said,
"What? I can't very well sleep in it! It's all I
brought to wear tomorrow."

He nodded in short jerky motions. "So just what
was your plan, anyway? I mean, besides the brilliant part about finding Gianni and killing him in
cold blood. What were you planning on doing after
that?"

She shrugged. "I hadn't thought that far ahead."

"You don't ever seem to think too far ahead, do
you?"

She rolled to face him. "What's that supposed to
mean?"

"Hell, Jasmine, think about it! First you run from
this guy, then you turn around without so much as
a so long and run right back to him again. What
the hell happened to make you change directions
on a dime like that?"

"I...I changed my mind."

"You changed your mind. First you're terrified
and in hiding, and then you're hunting the man

down, ready to blow him away. And you tell me you just changed your mind.''

She nodded hard. ''Why is that so hard to believe?''

He shook his head. ''Do you give any thought at all to these decisions of yours, or just act completely on impulse, doing whatever pops into your head at the time?''

''Of course I gave it thought! God, do you know how hard it was for me to leave Bax? To come back here to face a man I fully expected to do his best to kill me the minute he saw me?''

''Then why?''

She rolled away from him. ''For Baxter. He...he wants to stay in Quinn. I want him to have what he wants.''

He was silent for a long moment. ''And what about you, Jasmine? What do you want?''

''It's too late for what I want.'' She curled tighter around herself, closed her eyes. ''Just go to sleep now, Luke. It's late.''

He was silent. She kept her eyes closed, but his question lingered, whispered itself again and again in her mind. What did she want? It kept gnawing at her and eating at her until she couldn't keep the tears back anymore. And when they came, they came softly, quietly, and yet somehow, he knew.

A second later, his warm body curled around hers from behind. His arms came around her to hold her close. His breath came from close to her ear, and he said, "It's okay, Jasmine. Let it out. Talk to me. No one's here. No one ever needs to know. Just talk to me. Tell me what you want for you, what you think it's too late to have."

And it came out, all in a rush, with sobs and tears she hadn't meant to shed—especially not in front of a man. She wanted her mother—not the careless alcoholic who'd spent her nights in the arms of any man who would have her. The mother she'd dreamed about. One who loved her. Who held her and rocked her and brushed her hair and read her bedtime stories. She wanted her father. Not the one who'd knocked her mother up one night and left without a trace. But the one who would carry her around the house on his shoulders, and take her on camping trips and picnics. She wanted a childhood. Not the one she'd spent tiptoeing through the house in the mornings so as not to wake up her hungover mother and whatever stranger was in her bed. But a happy, loving one that only existed in her dreams.

Luke held her and stroked her hair and listened until the turmoil seemed to ease. And she relaxed against him. And she said, "More than anything else, I want those things for Baxter. All those things I never had. That happy, idyllic childhood. A home. A family." She bit her lip, closed her eyes. "And what have I given him? A mother who takes her clothes off for money. A front-row seat at a brutal murder. More fear and trauma than my lousy mother ever gave me, even at her worst. When I was so determined to be different. God, Luke, what have I done to my precious baby?"

"Jasmine, you've got it wrong. So wrong." Very gently, he rolled her over. She wore only her panties. Her chest was bare, and his arms were around her, holding her so close that their bodies touched all over. He tucked her head to his chest, and he rubbed his cheek over the top of her hair. "There's a big difference, and you're missing it by a mile. Baxter knows you love him. He knows you'd die for him without batting an eye. He knew when you left that you had come up here to try to protect him. And he knows you are always there for him, no matter what, because you love him more than anything else in the world. He knows that, Jasmine."

Her tears were wetting his chest. He didn't seem to mind. "Do you think he does?"

"He told me how you threw something at the shooter the day of the murder. He told me you did it so the man would shoot at you instead of him. He's a bright kid, Jasmine. Too bright not to know what's happening here. He'd rather be with you, on the run or wherever, than in some perfect home with a picket fence without you."

She tipped her head up, looked at his face. "But I wanted to give him that. The home, the picket fence..."

"You will. You will. You'll see. You're almost there already. There's this one last problem we need to get past, and then you'll see it all fall into place.

Jasmine, don't you think maybe this all happened for a reason? Don't you think maybe you were led to Quinn because it was where you and Baxter belong?''

She lowered her eyes. "I don't know. Your cousin Wes was saying something very similar. Maybe it's true."

"It's true." He closed his eyes. "It's true. The job, Ben and Penny deciding to hire a dance teacher just when you arrived…it's all fallen into place as if it were meant to be, Jasmine."

She nodded. "Maybe."

"What are you afraid of?" he asked her.

She closed her eyes. "That it's all a dream. Just like the dreams I had as a little girl. They're golden bubbles that shimmer and gleam and float in front of your eyes, and they seem so real. So beautiful. So perfect. But the moment you reach out to touch them, they burst, and there's nothing left. Not even the illusion. It hurts when that happens, Luke. I don't want to hurt like that again. And I don't want Baxter to ever hurt like that."

He held her closer, leaned in and kissed her forehead. "Then don't look at the bubble. Look past the dream, Jasmine, look at what's real. Quinn is real. The Brands are real, and they adore you and Baxter. The job offer from Ben and Penny, that's real. You can make a fresh start in Quinn. That's real. That's not an illusion. So reach for that. And don't worry about the rest. Not now."

She lifted her eyes to his, her hands at the back of his head, and she said, "And what about you...and me?"

He closed his eyes slowly, bit his lip. "I'm your friend, because that's what you need me to be right now."

"I don't think I've ever had a man who was a friend before."

"You do now."

She thought he must be lying. Because she was all but naked, and he was holding her tight in his arms right now, and he was all but naked, too, and it wasn't difficult to tell that he wanted her. All the evidence was there. He leaned down and kissed her lips, long and slowly, and so tenderly she trembled inside. She knew he wanted to make love to her. And she didn't mind. He'd done so much for her already. And she liked making love to him. The last time had been like nothing she'd ever known.

But when he lifted his head, he rolled further onto his back, cradling her to his chest. His hand stroked her hair, and he said, "Go to sleep, sweet Jasmine. I'm not gonna let any more bad dreams come near you tonight. You're safe now."

He was so warm around her. So firm beneath her. She closed her eyes as his hand stroked her hair over and over again. "I don't need any man to keep me safe," she whispered. "Never have. Never will." And then she snuggled closer.

Chapter 14

It was heaven and hell all rolled into one warm, beautiful female form in his arms that night. He didn't sleep. He just held her. Looked at her. And he knew, as he'd never known before, that he would do whatever it took to get through to her, to reach her. She had built a brick wall around her heart. He had to tear it down brick by brick. He had to get to her. Letting her go was no longer an option he cared to consider.

She began to stir when the morning sun slanted in through the window blinds, making yellow slashes of light across her face. She opened her eyes, blinked him into focus and then looked confused. He smiled at her, kissed her forehead, then rolled out of bed and walked around the room picking up his clothes. "I'm gonna get one of the guys over here to keep an eye on you while I shower," he said. "Okay?"

She nodded confusedly and, holding the blankets to her chest, tugged her own clothes off the foot of the bed and pulled them to her. "You didn't...I mean, you slept with me all night, and we didn't...."

"No," he said. "We didn't."

Tilting her head to one side, she said, "Why?"

Luke grinned at her. "Not because I wouldn't have liked to, believe me." But then he let the smile fade and went to sit on the edge of the bed. He stroked her hair, masses of it tangling around his fingers like coiled silk. "God, you've got the most incredible hair, you know that?" He drew a handful close to his face, inhaled its fragrance. Still fresh from her shower last night. But then he let it fall and looked her in the eyes. "I want to make sure you know that I feel something for you. Something that has nothing to do with sex. I'd feel it even if I knew you were never, ever going to let me make love to you again. And I also want you to know that when we did make love—it meant something to me. I don't want us to do it again until it means something to you, too."

She frowned very hard at him. "Means something...? What are you saying?"

"Well, I can't be sure, because I've never been

through this before. But as near as I can figure, I'm in love with you, Jasmine.''

She didn't react with a breathless sigh or a wavering smile. She didn't fall into his arms or cry or plaster his face with kisses. Instead, her eyes widened. She looked scared to death. ''You...you love me? But...you *can't*.''

''Oh, I'm pretty sure I can.'' He drew a breath, examining her face, realizing he'd shaken her up with that declaration. ''Look, I'm not expecting anything from you. This doesn't mean you have to say or do anything at all. Hell, I know you didn't need to hear this right now. To tell you the truth, I didn't intend to tell you until all this other stuff was behind us. But something made me go and let on anyway.''

Jasmine blinked slowly. Then she ducked underneath the covers and wriggled around under there, and when she came out again, her bra was in place, and her arms were in the sleeves of the white button-down shirt. He loved that she hid from him to dress. It was such a contradiction. He'd seen her undressed. She'd stripped for strangers, and now she ducked under the covers to get dressed. It was a quirk. And it told him she valued him more than she did those strangers. And that meant something to him. Besides, he loved her quirks.

When she emerged, that confused, puzzled frown was still on her face. She slipped out the other side of the bed, stood up with her back to him and slowly buttoned the shirt. "I don't get it," she said. "I don't have any real claim to your house. You know that now, right? It's going to auction next Saturday, just as planned and there won't be anything stopping you from buying it." She finished buttoning the shirt and reached for the jeans, then turned her back to him again and sat on the edge of the bed to pull them over her legs. "I don't have anything, you know. No money. Nothing of value. And I've got a kid, for crying out loud." She stood up, pulled the jeans over her hips and then snapped them, zipped them, faced him again. "I just don't get what's in this for you. Why would you want to fall in love with someone like me?"

He probably should have been insulted. But he knew she quite simply had no frame of reference for what he was trying to say to her. He put his own jeans on but didn't bother yet with the shirt. "I don't think people generally get a choice in the matter. You fall in love with someone for who they are, not what they have or what's in it for you. But maybe you can't really understand that until it happens to you. I mean, up until you came crashing into my life, I thought I was going to get to decide when, why, how and who I would love. But it doesn't happen that way, Jasmine."

She lowered her head, totally confused, by the looks of her. He said, "Will you stay put while I go next door and get one of the guys?"

"I'm not gonna run away, Luke. You don't have

to make one of your cousins guard me while you shower.''

He smiled. ''That's good to know.''

''What do you think we should do next?'' she asked.

Luke turned, and he couldn't help but feel it was good sign, her asking his opinion on this battle she'd been so determined to fight on her own up to now. ''I think we should take your tapes to the police, turn this whole mess over to them and go back to Texas where we belong.''

She shook her head slowly. ''I don't trust the police. Petronella's one of them.''

''Then we'll have Garrett contact the FBI. Hand the tapes over to them.''

''That's a little better.''

''Then that's what we'll do.'' He reached out, ran a finger down her cheek. He loved touching her. ''But until we're safely back home again, I'd still feel better if you weren't left alone too long.''

She sighed, but nodded. ''Fine. Go get the troops, then.''

Luke went to the door, opened it, and looked up and down the walk outside. The place was pretty silent this early in the morning. Nothing much stirred besides the light misty fog that had crept in overnight. He stepped outside, pulling the door closed behind him, and walked the few feet to the next door down, tapped on it. ''Ben? Garrett?''

He heard the door to Jasmine's room open and

glanced back down the sidewalk to see her there. She leaned out the door, her hair catching the breeze and dancing on it. "We should get coffee, Luke. Do you think the diner is open yet?"

Something moved in Luke's peripheral vision. A dark form swathed in the mists of the parking lot. Garrett opened the door and spoke, but Luke was turning away now, as that dark shape took the form of a man, and one arm rose slowly and pointed toward Jasmine. She couldn't see the man. There was no time to warn her.

Luke lunged as the distant arm came level. He threw himself between Jasmine and the gunman, and he never heard the bullets that hammered into his chest. But he felt them. They pounded and burned and tore, knocking him to the pavement as powerfully as if he'd been hit by a wrecking ball. Jasmine screamed. Garrett swore. The rest was a blur. What had been unfolding in slow motion suddenly jumped to fast forward. Jasmine fell to her knees at his side, leaning over him, crying. Her hands touched his chest and came away bloody. Her tears rained warm on his face. He didn't know where Garrett had gone. Ben was there, too, gently guiding Jasmine's hands back to Luke's chest, pressing them down on the wounds, instructing her to keep the pressure on. Luke didn't see the others. He heard footfalls in the parking lot, squealing tires. Everything had a distant, hollow sound to it—as if he were hearing it from the far end of a deep cave.

It occurred to him that there wasn't any pain now. That probably didn't bode well. Damn, he had things to do yet—for Jasmine, and for Baxter.

He forced his arm to move, lifted it, closed his hand on Ben's collar. "You're...my...witness."

"Don't try to talk, Luke. Take it easy, now. Help's on the way."

"God, what happened? What happened?" Jasmine was asking, choking on tears. "He's been shot. God, he's been shot."

"Ben..." Luke forced the words out, every one requiring tremendous effort. "Take the money. Buy the Walker place. For Jasmine."

"I understand, I got it, Luke, but please, stop talking now. I'm trying to keep you around long enough to see to all that yourself, so hush up."

Luke let his hand fall to the ground. He never felt it hit. He turned his gaze in search of Jasmine, whispered her name.

"I'm right here," she told him. And she moved so he could see her more clearly, but she still kept her hands pressed hard to his chest. "I'm right here, Luke."

He locked his eyes on her, held them there and knew she was unharmed. None of the bullets had reached her. Thank God, he thought. Thank God. "Go home," he told her. "Go home to Baxter." And then everything went dark. Her tears were the last thing he saw.

* * *

"Luke? Luke, come on? Don't fade on me now, come on! Luke?" Her entire body shook with tremors that seemed to come from down deep in her core. She leaned over Luke, her hands pressing hard to stop the blood pumping from his chest. He wasn't wearing a shirt, but his chest was slick with blood, and no matter how hard she pressed, it continued to seep out of him.

She understood what had happened. Luke had seen someone taking aim at her, out there in the misty parking lot somewhere. And he'd thrown himself into the line of fire. Like some kind of silver-screen hero. As if she were worth saving. He lay there on the concrete, blood all around him, under him, soaking through her jeans where she knelt beside him. Sirens wailed now, and all she could do was kneel beside Luke, her hands striving to keep the precious blood from flowing from his body. Her stomach heaved and clenched, and she felt dizzy. She had to battle the need to whirl away from him and throw up. He lay there, pale and still, his eyes closed now. Maybe he was dying. She didn't know. Maybe he was already dead. She couldn't stop trembling, sobbing. She hadn't felt this kind of panic hit her since that horrible day when she'd seen a man firing a gun at her own little boy. This sickening, gut-wrenching fear was the same. Except then, even as she'd sped away, she'd been able to see that Baxter was unharmed. This time, it was different. This time, the person she was so concerned for had holes torn through his body and blood streaming from the wounds.

"We got him!" someone called, and Ben looked up from what he was doing.

"Wes! Get over here and help me. We're gonna lose him if we can't stop this bleeding."

In a split second Wes Brand was kneeling opposite Ben. Jasmine had been paying little attention to what Ben was doing, but now she watched as his brother joined him. The two men moved their hands over Luke's body again and again. Wes muttered something in a low voice in a language that wasn't familiar to her. Comanche, she guessed. Jasmine wondered what earthly good they thought they were doing, but then the blood oozing from beneath her hands slowed. Her throat went dry. She thought she might be imagining things, but it slowed more. Maybe it only meant…no, no, Luke was still breathing. She lifted her gaze to the two brothers— their eyes were closed, their hands still moving. "Keep it up," she whispered. "Whatever you're doing, it's working. Keep it up."

The men didn't acknowledge her words. But she knew they heard. The blood flow eased more, and then it stopped—or she was pretty sure it stopped. She didn't dare take her hands away to check, but she couldn't see it flowing anymore, couldn't feel it pulsing against her hands, which were gloved now by the slick, glossy fluid.

Sirens screamed nearer. Men in white came with a gurney and cases full of supplies, and she was forced to move away from Luke. So were Wes and Ben. She got to her feet, staggering backward a few steps. For the first time she looked around her.

Dozens of people had gathered, forming a loose circle around the spot where Luke lay. Some were still in their nightclothes. They stared at her, shaking their heads, making sympathetic sounds as she scanned their faces. Dizziness, sickness, regret swamped her. Her world tilted, and her knees gave out. But a pair of arms closed around her waist before she could hit the pavement.

Wes held her easily upright. "Come on, let's get you someplace where you can sit."

"I have to go with Luke," she said. She lifted her gaze, blinking, not seeing anything clearly. Then Ben seemed to appear from nowhere a few feet away, clearing the crowd with a wave of his arms like Moses parting the Red Sea. Wes scooped her up and carried her back into motel room. Elliot appeared to open the door, so Wes could set her inside. Then Elliot handed her a bottle of water— she had no clue where he'd gotten it. But she sipped gratefully.

"Get her cleaned up and bring her on to the hospital," Elliot said. "I'll ride with Luke."

"No, I should go...." She tried to get to her feet, but her legs buckled.

"We'll be two minutes behind the ambulance, if

that. I promise,'' Wes said. He nodded to Elliot, who ran out the door, back to the ambulance. A second later she heard its siren howl as it sped away.

Ben came out of the bathroom with an ice bucket full of water and a washcloth. He dipped her hands into the water and gently washed them. She tried not to look at the water as it changed to the color of Luke's blood. Ben took it away, dumped it, brought back more. Then he peeled off her white blouse, ruined now, while Wes brought a fresh shirt for her. It was Luke's shirt, she realized as they put it on her, dressing her as if she were a helpless child. She lowered her head to cry, but paused when she saw the police cars outside.

Near the nose of the first car, Garrett was talking to several police officers, who held a handcuffed tough between them. The guy was stocky, dark and thoroughly battered. His face looked as if someone had used it for a punching bag. "Is that the man?" she asked. "Is he the one who shot Luke?"

"Yeah," Ben said. "Garrett, Elliot and Wes chased him down."

"He tossed the gun as he ran," Wes said. "Had a silencer on it, which is why we didn't hear the shots. Is that the guy who's been after you and Baxter all this time?"

She shook her head slowly. "No."

She lowered her head. Ben raised it again. He was back with a fresh washcloth, and he wiped her face now. She tried not to think about what was on it. He washed her neck, buttoned up Luke's shirt for her. "There. Almost as good as new. You have a fresh pair of jeans in here?"

She nodded vaguely. "Yeah. I can...I can do the rest."

Jasmine got to her feet, only to have Ben's arm instantly link with hers to help her to the bathroom. Inside, she peeled of her blood-soaked jeans, then sat on the edge of the bathtub and cranked on the water, washing her legs as it ran. She had to close her eyes. God, she couldn't bear much more. Poor Luke.

Getting to her feet, she dried off, pulled on the fresh jeans and turned toward the mirror.

The woman who looked back at her was a stranger. Jasmine wasn't even sure she recognized her. This was not the loner who trusted no one and thought of men as a baby step up the evolutionary ladder from dogs. This was not the street-tough city girl who could coldly strip for money and never let it get to her. This was not the woman who didn't believe in love.

She didn't know who the hell this woman in the mirror was. And that scared her.

There was a tap on the door. "You okay in there, hon?"

Ben's voice, deep with concern. She turned and opened the door. "I'm ready."

Flanked by Ben and Wes, she moved out of the motel room. The minute she was in sight, two of the cops outside came toward her. Garrett was with them. The suspect, the shooter, was at the second police car with a third cop, some fifty feet away.

Garrett said, "I know this is hard, hon, but we have to know. Do you know that man?" He pointed at the suspect. "Is this the guy you saw commit that murder at The Catwalk? The one who fired shots at you and your little boy?"

"No," she said. "That's not him. Gianni probably hired him to…ohmyGod." She came to a halt, and all eyes were on her. She was the only one looking toward the cop in the distance, who had put the shooter into the back of the car and was getting into the front. "That's him…that's the killer!"

"It is the same guy, after all?" Garrett asked as the patrol car rolled around the diner, toward the highway.

"Not the shooter. The cop. That's him. That cop is the killer!"

All eyes turned toward the patrol car as it merged into traffic, picked up speed.

The two officers tensed, looking at each other in confusion, and one of them said, "That's Officer Petronella, ma'am. Are you sure about this?"

"That is the man who tried to kill my son and shot at me. That's the man I saw murder the undercover agent at The Catwalk. I have his confession on audio and videotape, back in the motel room." Ben headed back to get them even as she went on. "And if you get him behind a two-way mirror, I can promise you Leo, the bar's owner, will identify him, too.''

"Didn't I tell you he was dirty?" one cop said to the other. "We'd better get to this Leo fellow before Gianni does." He keyed a microphone clipped to his collar and started speaking into it as he headed for his car.

"I'm more worried about that suspect right now," the other cop said. "If he worked for Petronella, he can testify to that in court. Hell, he'll never make it to the station." He looked at Garrett, then at Jasmine. "There's still a warrant out for your arrest, ma'am."

"I'll keep her and the evidence in my custody," Garrett said. "When you're ready to take her statement and the tapes, we'll be at the hospital. But I promise you, once you do, that warrant will be dropped."

The cop nodded. "She's your responsibility, Sheriff Brand. Don't leave town until this is settled. Understand?"

Jasmine nodded. Then she and the others went to Ben's SUV and piled in. Garrett got behind the wheel, and as they sped toward the hospital, he said, "I just hope to hell they catch that bastard."

Jasmine hovered outside the doors of the room marked Trauma 1, trying to see beyond the mesh-lined safety glass and the sea-green lab coats that surrounded Luke. A pretty young nurse touched her shoulder and said, "Come to the waiting room, miss. You'll be so much more comfortable there."

"I'm *not* moving!" She didn't speak the words so much as bark them. It was at least the fourth time the perky blonde had bothered her.

"Easy, Jazz. She's just trying to help." It was Wes's voice. He had a cup of coffee in one hand, and he sent the nurse an apologetic glance that told her it was all right, he would handle things. The nurse sighed and moved away. Wes came closer, pressed the cup into Jasmine's hand, looked past her at the windows, and saw no more than she'd been able to see before.

"You and Ben ought to be in there," Jasmine muttered. "You could probably do as well as they are."

He shook his head. "They know what they're doing. This is Chicago. They know how to take care of gunshot wounds here."

"It's been an hour."

"It might be two. You sure you don't want to come sit with us?"

She shook her head, sighed, sipped the coffee. "What was that, anyway? What you and Ben were doing back there to make the bleeding stop the way you did?"

Wes shrugged. "I think Ben calls it reiki. He studied lots of Eastern mysticism along with martial arts a while back. Still keeps up with most of it. As for my part, I was just using an old Comanche healing technique. I think it's pretty much the same thing, either way.''

"It was amazing.''

Wes shrugged. "Actually, stopping blood is fairly easy. I'll show you sometime.''

"I'd like that.'' She turned to peer through the window again.

"He's gonna be all right, Jasmine.''

She closed her eyes, lowered her head. "Why did he do it, Wes? Why did he jump in front of me like that? What the hell could he possibly have been thinking?''

Wes frowned at her as if she were asking an inane question. "He was trying to protect you.''

"By getting himself shot? God, Wes, I just don't get it. Who does something like that for someone else? And why, for God's sake?''

He just looked at her for a long moment. Then he said, "You remember when you saw Petronella shooting at Baxter? What did you do?''

She paced away from the door, shaking her head. "I threw something at him, yelled at him, waved my arms.''

"Why?''

"*Why?* To distract his attention away from my son, so he wouldn't shoot him.''

"And didn't it occur to you that the man would only shoot at you instead?'' Wes asked.

"I *knew* he would shoot at me instead. But it didn't matter. I mean, better me than Baxter.''

Wes came to where she stood, put a hand on her shoulder. "And why would you be willing to risk your own life in order to save Baxter's?"

She blinked. "Well...I'm his mother."

"Oh. Well. If that's all it was... Would your mother have done that for you, do you think?"

"Shoot, my mother would have used me for a shield, given the chance." She licked her lips, lowered her head. "But I'm not like her. I love my baby. I'd do anything for him. There's nothing in the world more important to me than that child, not even my own life. I'd die for him in a heartbeat and never once regret it. That's how much I love him."

She finished speaking, lifted her head slowly. And Wes held her gaze and nodded slowly. "And that's how much Luke loves you."

It was like a flash of light in her eyes that was so bright it blinded her. The pain in her chest doubled, and for a second she couldn't breathe. She actually staggered backward as if Wes had delivered a physical blow. One hand pressed to her heart in a knee-jerk reaction, and she leaned against the wall behind her.

The double doors opened. People in green rushed out, wheeling Luke on the gurney amid them. One pushed an IV pole with bags swinging and tubes attached to Luke's arms.

"Are you family?" a male doctor asked her. She

brushed him aside and tried to run along beside the gurney.

"I am," Wes told the doctor.

The gurney stopped at an elevator, and a nurse hit the button. Jasmine crowded her way between the people and leaned over Luke. God, he was so still, so very white. A sheet covered him from the hips down, and his chest was patched with bloody squares. Tubes in his nose. Tubes in his arms.

"Luke...?" Jasmine whispered.

The elevator doors opened. A nurse touched her arm. "We have to take him up to surgery now. Sixth floor. There's a waiting room up there. We're going to do everything we can, I promise you."

"Luke!"

They pushed him past her, into the elevator, as she stretched her hands out toward him, as if she could hold on to him somehow. Then the doors closed, and she stood there, staring. It wasn't possible that a man like Luke could love her the way Wes said he did. No one in her life had ever loved her like that. Well, no one except for Bax. But he had to love her. She was his mom. My God, the sheer magnitude of this was more than her mind could wrap itself around all at once. How could he love her that much? How could *anyone* love her that much? What the hell did she have that made her deserve it? And yet, it must be true. Because the man had dived in front of bullets for her. *He'd dived in front of bullets for her!* Shielded her with his own body. Knowing damn well he would be shot instead.

Who *did* things like that?

"Jasmine?"

She lifted her head, blinked at Wes.

"She looks shocky, Wes. Maybe we should get a doc to take a look at her," Elliot said.

"You all right, Jazz?"

She tipped her head to one side. When had Wes taken to calling her that? When had she decided she liked it? Why did it make her feel like part of his family? "They...have to operate on him," she said. "Sixth floor. We should go up."

Wes nodded. Garrett turned and punched the elevator button, and they stood there, waiting. "So what did they say to you, Wes?" Garrett asked.

"They needed the consent of a family member. That's all."

The doors opened; they all stepped inside. Jasmine watched Wes's face and saw his eyes. There was more. "That's not all," she said. "Tell us, Wes. I already know it's bad. That nurse told me they'd do everything they could. I know what that means as well as anyone. It means they're not sure they can save him."

Wes lowered his head. When he lifted it again, he glanced at Garrett, and Garrett nodded. "She's tougher than she looks. You might as well tell us the worst of it, Wes."

Swallowing hard, Wes said, "One bullet went

clear through, punctured a lung on the way. That's bad enough, but the second one is still inside him. It damaged his heart and lodged in his back—it's near his spine. They need to get it out, because if it shifts position it could kill him or cripple him. There's no telling yet how much damage it's already done. They need to repair the tear to his heart and get that bullet out of his spine. Then they'll work on the lung.''

The doors opened again. For a minute Jasmine couldn't even move. Garrett had to take her arm and push her along to get her going. Her feet came down then, one in front of the other, but she wasn't directing them.

Ben said, ''Has anyone called home?''

''Yeah,'' Garrett said. ''But it's time for an update.'' He pulled the cell phone out of his pocket.

''I want to talk to Baxter,'' Jasmine said softly.

''That's good, that'll help him feel better.''

''I don't know how. I can't tell him Luke will be okay. I can't tell him Petronella has been caught and locked up where he can't hurt us anymore. The only thing I can tell him is…that I'm sorry. I'm sorry I got the only man that boy has ever loved shot.'' She lifted her eyes, looking at each of the men in turn. ''And I need to tell you that, too. And your whole family. I'm sorry. I'm so damn sorry I ever darkened your door and brought all this trouble down on you. It's my fault Luke's lying in there fighting for his life. My fault. I wish I could take it back.''

Wes shook his head at her. ''Luke wouldn't have had it any other way, you know. If he had it to do over, he'd do it just the same.''

She closed her eyes and, finally, let Ben lead her to a chair.

Chapter 15

"I think he's coming around," a voice said. It was a gentle voice, a familiar one. Luke was struggling to stay afloat in a very deep, very dark sea, but waves kept pushing him under again. Then a hand closed around his, and he gripped it as if it were his lifeline.

"I'm right here, Luke. I'm right here."

Slowly he blinked his eyes open. "Jasmine...?"

"Right here," she said. He sought her out with his eyes, found her. She was a blur, but gradually she came into focus. She didn't look well. She was pale, and her hair was hanging in a limp ponytail with many strands dangling free. No makeup. She had red-rimmed, puffy eyes.

"You okay?" he asked weakly. God, why was it so much effort to put words together?

"Am *I* okay?" She smiled, but sadly. "I'm fine. You're the one who got himself shot."

He frowned. Shot? It took moments of intense concentration to make sense of her words. Then, finally, he remembered. "Did they get him?"

"Yeah. They got him."

"And? What else?" he asked her.

She said, "It wasn't Petronella. Just one of his flunkies. Petronella took off with him before I could ID him. Bastard had the nerve to show up at the scene. But it's gonna be okay. The police tracked him down in short order. He'd already shot his flunky and dumped the body alongside the highway. He's in custody now. They have my tapes— but I made copies first, just in case. I'm in the clear, and there's plenty of evidence to send Petronella up for life. It's all going to be okay. Finally."

He sighed his relief. Thank God the risk to Jasmine was ended. They'd gotten the bastard. He swallowed hard. Then Jasmine leaned over him, cupping his head with her soft hand and lifting his head just a little, holding a glass of water with a straw to his lips. He drank, then she lowered his head gently back against the pillows again. "Damn, I'm weak. How bad off am I?"

"You're gonna be fine," she told him, setting the water down. But she wasn't facing him when she said it.

"Jasmine?"

She turned, sat on the edge of his bed, pressed

her hands to his cheeks and said, "You're okay. We almost lost you, Luke, but you're okay now. They operated in Chicago. They said it went well, but they wanted to keep you out for a little while. There was some damage to your spine—nothing serious or permanent. One of the bullets came close, though. They didn't want you even trying to move until you'd had a couple days to let the healing process take hold."

He blinked in shock, trying to take stock of his body, especially his legs and feet. They felt odd. Heavy and tingling, as if they'd gone to sleep. But he could feel them, at least. "How long have I been unconscious?" he asked.

"Two days. This morning they shipped you back here, to El Paso, and took you off sedation. You're back in Texas, Luke. We've been here a whole hour already."

He closed his eyes, feeling an inexplicable surge of contentment wash through him like a warm tide. Hell, whatever happened, he could handle it here. Home. Texas. He really had sunk his roots into the Texas soil, then, hadn't he?

There was a tap on the door. Then it opened. "Doc said he was coming around," Chelsea said, poking her head inside. "I brought a visitor."

The door opened wider, and Baxter came in, almost tiptoeing, his eyes wide and worried.

Jasmine gulped back a sob and ran to her son. She scooped him right up and held him tight, covering his little face with her kisses. "Oh, Bax, honey, I missed you so much!"

"Me too, Mom," he said, hugging her neck.

In the bed, Luke's throat closed up tight, and his eyes burned.

"Thanks for bringing him, Chelsea. I couldn't wait, and I couldn't leave, and I just…thank you."

"Hey, I'd have come whether you asked me to or not. Heck, the whole clan is out there waiting to see Luke. But I'll give the three of you some time first." She ducked back outside, and pulled the door closed behind her.

"Luke?" Baxter asked softly. He squirmed out of his mother's arms, went to the chair and pulled it up close to the bed. Then he climbed up. "You okay?"

"They tell me I'm gonna be just fine, kiddo. Nothing to worry about."

Very gently, Bax reached out and hugged Luke's neck. "You kept your promise," he said. "Just like you said you would. You brought my mom back home."

"Told you, kid. I never break a promise." Luke made the effort it took to put his arms around Bax and hug him in return, but damn, it was hard work.

"I love you, Luke," Baxter said.

Oh, hell, that did it. His eyes didn't just burn now, they welled to overflowing, despite Luke's rapid blinking. "I love you, too, Bax."

* * *

Jasmine stood there and watched the two embrace. She saw the tears in Luke's eyes and the adoration in Baxter's. And all of the sudden, she needed to be alone. She was so close to something. So close to finally understanding…it was nipping at her brain, and she just needed to grab hold of it and hold on.

She backed out of the room. The two were so involved with each other by then, she didn't think either of them would notice. She ran right past the crowd of Brands lingering in the hall, located the nearest rest room and ducked inside. She cranked on the cold water tap, splashed handfuls of it in her face, battled an attack of hyperventilation.

Both hands braced on the sink, she lifted her head and stared into the mirror. "My God," she whispered. "You love him. You love that man!"

Chelsea sat by the bedside. "Stop worrying, Luke. She only went to the rest room."

Luke frowned anyway, worried all the same. "She didn't look well, Chelsea." Baxter had curled up beside him on the bed, snuggled into a little ball in the crook of his arm, and fallen asleep.

"Well, *of course* she didn't. She's been holding a vigil at your bedside since you came out of surgery. They couldn't get her to leave. She flew home with you. The girl's got it bad, Luke."

He shook his head. "She feels responsible, I imagine. It's just guilt."

Chelsea smiled. "Ah, be dense if you want to. Why mess up a perfectly good Brand family tradition?"

He sent her a smirk. "How come Garrett's not with you?"

"The menfolk had to take off. Got a call from a neighbor. Seems the north pasture fence is down and we have cattle all over the place. They won't be long getting things squared away."

He nodded. There was yet another tap on the door, and a nurse came in. "We have to take Mr. Brand down to X-ray now. It won't take long."

Chelsea nodded, got to her feet and gathered Baxter up in her arms. "See you in a few minutes, Luke."

"Thanks, Chelsea. For taking such good care of Bax and…and, well, everything."

She nodded. "A fall wedding would be nice, don't you think?" She sent him a wink and carried Bax out into the waiting room.

Luke lay back, thinking his cousin-in-law had higher hopes than he did. Damn, a fall wedding sounded good to him, too, though. He smiled crookedly as the nurse wheeled him out of his room, into an elevator. Then she pulled a needle out of a deep white pocket.

"What's that?" he asked. "Not more sedatives, I hope. I'd like to stay awake for a while."

The nurse smiled down at him. "Just pain meds. Don't worry." She stuck the needle into his IV tube. A second ticked by, then two, and then his head was swimming.

"Whoa, those must be powerful…main peds…uh…I mean um…" He forgot what he'd been saying. The doors slid open, and she pushed him out. Ceiling lights flashed overhead, running past him as if they were attached to a conveyor belt. He found that incredibly funny and started to laugh, but it hurt when he laughed, and he wondered vaguely why his pain meds didn't prevent that.

Doors whooshed open. Fresh Texas air hit him in the face. Hey, he was outdoors. Since when did they put X-ray outdoors? Whoa, now his bed was being picked up. What the hell? He tried to lift his head, to make sense of what he was seeing before the ambulance doors slammed shut on him. A man, handing a wad of cash to the nurse. The nurse, yanking off her name tag and tossing it onto the ground, then hurrying away. Hell, she was no nurse at all.

Still not sure who this woman was she had become—or was in the process of becoming—Jasmine left the rest room and went back to the waiting area where the Brand women were gathered. Chelsea said, "They had to take Luke down for an X-ray. He'll be back in a minute."

"God, talk about padding the bill," Jasmine muttered. "They just X-rayed the poor man a few minutes before you all got here."

Jessi said, "He'll be glowing in the dark if they keep this up." The others laughed. Kirsten and Penny. And the two women due to give birth at any moment, Taylor and Esmeralda.

Frowning, Jasmine said, "Where'd all your husbands go?"

"Had a cattle emergency out at the ranch," Chelsea said. "I'm sure they won't be long."

"Oh." Jasmine sat down, drumming her fingers on the arm of the overstuffed chair and glancing down the hall toward X-ray.

Then Chelsea's cell phone rang. She answered it and said, "No, Garrett's not available at the moment. This is his wife, can I take a message?" She listened, and her gaze flew to Jasmine's. "Oh, no."

"What?" Jasmine demanded.

Chelsea disconnected and eyed her. "Petronella's escaped. And the tapes you gave the police have vanished from the evidence room."

"Excuse me, ladies?" a deep voice said. They turned to see the swarthy Mexican-American physician they all called Doc standing there by Luke's hospital room door. "Can someone tell me where my patient has gone?"

"Oh, my God," Jasmine whispered. She whirled on Chelsea. "Which way did that nurse take Luke?"

"To the elevator—I think it was going down. Why?"

"Because X-ray is down the hall."

Chelsea frowned, looking from the doctor to Jasmine over and over. "You mean...you think..."

"I think Petronella somehow followed us here, and now he has Luke." Jasmine got to her feet, turned toward the elevator. "He probably even engineered that so-called emergency that got all the men out of the way."

"Wait!" Chelsea cried. "Jasmine, where the hell are you going?"

"I'm going after Luke!"

Chelsea caught her, gripped her shoulder, turned her around. "Not alone, you're not. That's not the way we do things in this family, Jasmine. You can't keep behaving like this loner you used to be, because that's not who you are anymore!"

"I'm not?" she asked, her tone impatient, even bordering on sarcastic.

"No. You're a Brand woman now. Maybe it's not official yet, but it's inevitable, and family means more than some legal documentation, anyway. You're one of us. So is Bax. And so is Luke. And Brands don't let family handle trouble alone."

For an instant, just an instant, she reeled at the power with which those words hit her. It was as if, suddenly, she knew it was utterly true. That was who she'd seen when she'd looked into the mirror. A woman who was part of a family. The family the child inside her had always longed for.

She was a Brand.

"Taylor and Esmeralda, you are far too pregnant

to be on this end of things. Take care of Baxter. Have Doc show you someplace safe to hole up, and insist some security people stay with you." She tossed the cell phone to Esmeralda, who caught it, frowned at it and handed it to Taylor. "Try to contact the men and tell them what's happened."

Doc was at the nurses' desk now, giving rapid orders. He turned and came toward Jasmine as she started for the elevator again. "An ambulance just pulled out of the lot, without its crew. And someone left this note for you at the desk."

He handed her a sealed envelope. She tore it open and read the note inside.

"Jasmine—If you want Luke Brand back alive, meet me when and where I say. Bring the original tapes, as I know full well those I stole were copies, and bring the boy. No one else, or your hero dies. Call this number in one hour for further instructions." It was signed GP.

She nodded. The elevator doors slid open, and she stepped inside. "The note says I'm to come alone," she said.

"Right," Chelsea replied. Then she, Jessi, Penny and Kirsten joined her. As the door slid closed again, Jasmine saw Taylor and Esmeralda being led down a hall by Doc, who carried a still sleepy Baxter.

Five women got out of the elevator on the ground floor and into Chelsea's station wagon. After asking which way the stolen ambulance had gone, Jasmine drove, and Chelsea read the note aloud to the others as they sped down the highway out of El Paso.

Kirsten smiled. "That's the good thing about small towns, you know? Not that many phone numbers. Even fewer exchanges. That one in particular belongs to a little town between El Paso and Quinn, right on the Rio Grande. It's called Deadrock, and I don't imagine it has too many public telephones."

"Chances are this Petronella character wouldn't be using a private one. He can't know anyone from around here, can he?"

"Doubtful," Jasmine said. "But why wouldn't he have just used his cell phone?"

"In Deadrock?" Kirsten smiled slowly. "No reception whatsoever."

Chelsea nodded slowly. "If he's in a motel and we call, we might get the front desk first, then we'll know where he is. Either way, I don't like the idea of waiting an hour. Why don't we call him back right now?"

"'Cause you gave your cell phone to Taylor," Jessi said.

Kirsten opened her designer handbag. "You think I leave home without one?" Then she frowned. "Should we call in the police on this?"

"And risk Luke's life?" Jasmine said, quickly and sharply. She schooled her tone before continuing. "No. We can call Garrett, tell him and the others where we're heading, but I don't think we should bring in any authorities. Not yet.'' She looked to Chelsea, a question in her eyes.

Chelsea nodded in agreement. ''We'll handle this the way we handle every other crisis—as a family. The men will be along as fast as they can get here. But we have a head start on catching up to this maniac. I have to believe we're the best chance Luke has right now.'' She looked around at the other women. ''So we go after him ourselves. Now. We don't wait. Agreed?''

One by one, the Brand women nodded.

Chapter 16

When Luke opened his eyes again, he was hurting big time. The pain was like a trail of fire, burning in his chest and his back. Hell, he couldn't even move without inducing more of it. And his legs tingled as if covered in fire ants. What the hell had happened? Where was he?

Warily he took in his surroundings, moving only his eyes, teeth grated. Paneled walls. A simple white globe of a light fixture in the ceiling. Cheesy art on the opposite walls. A window to the left—shade drawn, curtain closed so no light could stream in. He could only see the top of it without turning his head to see more. He was not in the hospital anymore.

And finally, a voice—from another room he

thought. The scent of tobacco smoke drifted on the air.

"I told you to call in an hour. Why are you early?" There was silence. Then, "If you can't obey simple instructions, maybe I should kill him and get the hell out of here."

Luke strained to lift his head. The spears of pain the act sent bolting through him were almost enough to make him scream aloud. But he forced it all the same and saw through the doorway into a second room, where a man sat at a table, smoking and speaking on the telephone.

"Fine. But this is your last chance, Jasmine. You bring the boy, and you bring the tapes, or your boyfriend here dies." He paused, flicked ashes onto the floor and nodded. "That's better. Now, there's a stretch of ground without much on it besides cactus and rock, twenty-one point five miles out of El Paso, heading west on 375. Only thing close is a billboard advertising the county fair. You know where I mean?" He nodded. "Good. That's where I'll be. Half hour. And, Jasmine? Don't bother trying to track me down through the phone number. I'll be long gone from here within minutes, and you'll only be wasting precious seconds of your boyfriend's life." He hung up the phone.

"You don't want those tapes, Petronella," Luke said, and it was a strain to say it. His voice came out gruff and hoarse. "You don't have any need of them now. Everyone knows you're guilty."

He shrugged. "Knowing it and proving it are two different things."

"You killed the guy who shot me," Luke went on.

"That's right, I did. Killed him with his own gun. For you, though, I'm gonna use mine. It hasn't had a good workout since before I was arrested. I had to tuck it into hiding fast, to keep the cops from confiscating it." He patted his side. His jacket hid the gun from view.

"So you've got two murder raps, and the escape charge to boot. Don't you see the tapes are of no use to you now?" Luke asked. "The only thing you can do now is run. You can never go back, even if you have the tapes."

Petronella got to his feet and walked slowly into the room where Luke was. He smoked slowly, thoughtfully. "You're too smart for your own good, you know that?"

"You don't want the tapes at all, do you?"

Petronella thrust out a lower lip. "Nah. I want revenge. The bitch messed up my life, and she's gonna pay. And there ain't a thing you can do about it, being laid up like you are. You can't even get out of that bed."

Luke wanted to leap out of the bed and nail the guy right then and there, but he could barely move. And then he thought maybe it was better to let Petronella go on believing he couldn't move at all. Even screaming pain was better than the numbness he'd felt before. But he would need every advantage.

"You're so close to the border, you know. You could walk out of here right now, cross the Rio Grande and be in Mexico. They'd never find you there. People get lost there all the time."

He nodded slowly. "That's the plan. Right after I off Jasmine and her scrawny kid, that's what I'll do. But first..." He reached into his jacket, pulled his gun level and aimed it at Luke. Luke tensed, preparing to lunge at the bastard with everything in him. But Petronella didn't fire. He frowned, looked at his gun, hefting it in his hand, his frown growing. "What the hell?" he asked, checking it, turning it over.

Luke almost went limp with relief when he saw that there was no clip in the gun's hollow handle. Petronella spewed a stream of obscenities. "Dammit, I don't have freaking time for this kind of— did you do this? Where the hell is my clip?" As he spoke, he worked the action of the gun. A single bullet popped out of the chamber and landed on the floor, rolling slowly.

One bullet.

Luke rolled out of the bed as Petronella reached for it. He landed hard, the bullet under him. Petronella gripped his shoulder, flung him onto his back.

Luke closed his hand around the bullet. "What's the matter, Gianni? Is it your last one?"

"It'll have to be enough. Gimme the bullet," Petronella demanded.

Luke lay on his back on the floor. "No freaking way."

"You think so, huh?" Petronella picked up a booted foot and stomped down hard on Luke's chest, right over one of the bullet wounds.

Pain hit him so hard he howled with it, but he didn't let go of the bullet. Arms crossed over his chest, he rolled onto his side, doubled in pain.

Petronella knelt in front of him. "Give it to me!"

Luke decked him—just poked upward and outward with a fist and all the power he could put behind it. Which wasn't a hell of a lot, he thought, but apparently it was enough to knock Petronella on his ass.

While the man was down, Luke rolled onto his belly, dragging himself, elbow over elbow, to the small room he'd spotted. He heard Petronella swear, heard him get up, and crawled faster. His upper body crossed the threshold. Petronella stepped down on the middle of Luke's back.

"Give me the effing bullet!"

Luke's back arched, chin coming off the floor in response to the weight on his injured back. The bastard would cripple him! He looked at the toilet ahead of him, lifted his arm, took careful aim despite the pain racking him—and let fly.

The small, shiny bullet flew in a perfect arc and hit the water with an anticlimactic little plop.

Petronella kicked him in the head, and Luke saw stars as the man walked over him to the toilet, and bent to thrust his hand into the water. Luke tried to move. And found he couldn't. Not at all. More interestingly than that, he couldn't feel much of anything anymore, either.

"Calling early didn't do a hell of a lot of good. I was hoping it was a pay phone or a motel, and someone else would answer. Someone who'd tell us where the phone was," Kirsten said after Jasmine's call to Petronella.

They'd stopped at a phone booth as they passed, just long enough for Chelsea to jump out, rip the telephone directory from its chain and jump back into the car again. Jessi was flipping through it now as they drove.

"I have it!" she said. "Shoot, it wasn't hard. Deadwood only takes up three pages. That number is for one of the rooms above the Deadwood Bar and Grill."

"Which is dead opposite the direction we need to head to meet Petronella," Chelsea pointed out. "If we go back, it'll make us late."

Jasmine shook her head. "And that could cost Luke his life. We have to make that meeting, Chelsea."

"I agree."

Jessi nodded hard. "Me too."

All the others in the car chimed in with agreement.

Jasmine thinned her lips. "You know as well as I do that Petronella probably won't keep his side of the bargain. Even if we do everything he wants."

"Fortunately," Chelsea said, reaching over to give Jasmine's hand a squeeze, "we aren't going to leave that decision up to him."

They reached the designated meeting place within minutes, since they were already nearly there. There was no significant cover around. Just a billboard, some cacti dotting the landscape, a tumbleweed here and there. "We haven't got any weapons," Kirsten said as Chelsea pulled the car to a stop along the roadside in a cloud of dust.

"I do," Jasmine said. She tugged her gun out of her handbag.

"Hell, we all do," Jessi put in. She got out of the station wagon, crouched down, and when she rose again, she was tossing a decent-sized rock in her hand. The others got out, too, gathered around her, nodded. "Best give one of us the gun, Jasmine," Jessi said. "He'll probably search you, if he gets the chance. Besides, we're gonna need him alive, unless he brings Luke with him."

Jasmine closed her eyes tight. "God, Luke wasn't even supposed to be moving around much. And he missed his pain meds." It turned her stomach to think of the pain he must be in right now.

To think of what Petronella might have done to him.

"Luke's a Brand, Jasmine. He's tough as they come. He's gonna come through this all right," Jessi said.

"Come on, let's find cover and weapons. Set this up right under and around that billboard. Best spot possible."

"I don't see how we're supposed to find any cover out here," Jasmine said, squinting, shading her eyes with her hand. A cactus, a tumbleweed, the car, which he would surely search, and the billboard itself, were all she saw.

Jessi smiled and patted her on the back. "Yeah, but you're from out of town. Come on hon. Let us show you how we do things in Texas."

Kirsten pulled a pair of imitation calfskin gloves out of her designer bag, and slipped her hands into them. Then she walked right up to a cactus, broke off one of its arms and swung it a few times like a club, nodding in satisfaction. "Bastard's gonna wish he hadn't started up with us," she muttered.

The half hour ticked by slower than molasses on a midwinter day. But Jasmine was ready. Following Jessi's instructions, she'd snapped a handful of tangles off the tumbleweed and brushed away all the footprints that showed anywhere. Mostly the ground here was hard packed and barren. The desert wasn't all sand, the way she'd always thought.

Then she stood in plain sight underneath the bill-board and waited.

Finally another car pulled to a stop alongside hers. Petronella sat still for a moment, looking around, listening. Then he got out, with his gun in hand. He strode right up to Chelsea's station wagon, opened its doors, searched inside it, then, satisfied, he looked up and down the road, and finally, walked off the pavement to where Jasmine waited, under the billboard, a hot, dry breeze raking her cheeks.

"I don't see the boy," he said.

"I didn't see any reason to bring him. You want the tapes. I want Luke. My son has nothing to do with it."

He shrugged. "Hell, I've only got one bullet on me anyway." He lifted the gun.

"Kill me and you won't get the tapes," she said, trying hard to hide the bolt of fear that jolted up her spine just then.

He smiled slowly. "Tapes aren't gonna do me any good anyway, sugar."

He smiled slowly, and his hand flexed on the gun so fast there was no time to do anything to prevent it. But only a dull click resulted when he pulled the trigger. Then Chelsea came hurtling down from the billboard where she'd been hiding—she'd had to stand on Jessi's shoulders to get hold of the sign's frame and had pulled herself up from there, clung to the back and waited for her moment. And it was perfect. She landed on top of Petronella, flattening him to the ground. He hit hard, but rolled over, flinging Chelsea off him. Kirsten leaped out from behind the one-armed cactus and smashed him in the face with her makeshift prickly club. He howled in agony, but already Jessi had shot out from where she'd been lying flat underneath the car and Penny rose up from under the tumbleweed. So when Petronella knocked Kirsten's club away and sat up with his hands to his face, it was only to get pegged by two cobble-sized stones, one from in front and one from behind.

He never stood a chance. His head was split open and bleeding in the back, swollen and purple on the front, and his face was extremely messed up, courtesy of the cactus. He never even got back on his feet again.

Jasmine yanked off her belt and tossed it to Jessi. Jessi knelt behind him and bound his hands. Then she tossed the gun back to Jasmine. "Your gun misfired," Jasmine said. "Mine won't. Where is Luke?"

He shook his head. "Damned wet powder," he muttered. "You can blow me away. I'll never tell you. You can just suffer for what you did. I can guarantee you he is—and the longer it takes you to find him, the better his chances of being dead before you do." He spat.

Jasmine pursed her lips. Jessi reached around the man from behind, grabbed his shirt by either side and tore it open, laying his chest and stomach bare. "Hey, Kirsten!" she called. "What'd you do with that cactus limb?"

"Oh, hell, Jessi, you don't want to beat the poor man with that thing," Chelsea said. "Not *there,* anyway." She nodded to Jasmine. "Let's yank off his pants. I mean, I think he'll talk faster."

Kirsten retrieved her limb and came forward, brushing it lightly over his chest, cactus spines raking his flesh. "Where did you leave Luke? Is he in that room you rented above the bar? Hmm?" She reached for his fly.

"Yes!" he shouted. Then, as she drew the club away, "How the hell did you know about the room?"

"City slicker," Jessi said. "You're clueless."

A huge pickup truck came skidding to a stop, sending up more dust clouds, and Brand men piled out of both doors and the back. They came running, then stopped and looked at the scene before them.

"You guys handle it from here," Jasmine said. "I'm going to find Luke."

"We'll send an ambulance, Jasmine," someone called.

She jumped in Chelsea's car and sped away.

She burst into the front part of the room, saw no one and raced through it, calling Luke's name. When she reached the bedroom she found him. He lay facedown on the floor, halfway into the small bathroom. His head was cut open, bleeding. His face was beaded with sweat and contorted in pain, and his eyes were squeezed shut tight.

She was beside him instantly. "Luke! It's all right. Hold on. Help is coming."

His eyes opened. He peered up at her. "You're alive...."

"Of course I'm alive. And Petronella's lucky to be. God, baby, what did he do to you?" She stroked his face, then dashed over him into the bathroom for a wet cool cloth. She wiped his face with it, then pressed it gently to the cut. "You have to be okay, Luke. Dammit, you have to be okay."

He smiled. "Doesn't matter. Just as long as you and Bax are."

She shook her head. "We won't be. Not if we don't have you."

His face changed. He looked surprised, but then something else. "Jasmine, even if I make it, I don't know...what I mean—I can't feel my legs, Jasmine. Not even a little."

"I love you, Luke," she whispered. "I finally understand what you were trying to tell me back there. I love you. Totally. I never thought I could feel this way for any man, but I do, and dammit, you promised me you'd help me start a new life. And I want that, Luke. I want to marry you. I want you to be a father to Baxter. I want that. Do you understand? So you just have to hang in there, Luke. You just have to. You *have to*."

He managed to smile, even past all the pain. "Well, hell, Jasmine, I couldn't die now if I wanted to. Not with an offer like that on the table."

Epilogue

"Welcome Home, Luke" the banner read, when Garrett and Wes pulled up at the brick house that had been known as the old Walker place. It wasn't anymore. The title now read Luke and Jasmine Brand.

Everyone had gathered for the celebration of Luke's release from the hospital. God, it had been three entire weeks. The physical therapy had been brutal and was ongoing. But he was getting better.

Mostly because of Jasmine.

She stood on the porch now, little Baxter in front of her, her hands on his shoulders. They both smiled widely as he got out of the pickup and limped up the walk. He carried a canvas tote in his free hand and leaned heavily on the cane that looked as if it was going to be his walking partner for a long time to come. Maybe forever.

He didn't give a damn. He had what mattered. Jasmine had married him in the hospital room. She'd refused to wait. The legal matters had taken longer, but Luke had had a visit from his lawyer today, just before his release, and now that part, too, was official.

Beyond Jasmine, the house was alive. He could see his family peering out every window and door, their smiles as bright as the happy tears in their eyes. They loved him. They loved her, too.

He made it to the steps, glanced at Garrett and Wes, who'd flanked him all the way, the overprotective lugs. "Can you keep them all at bay for just a sec?" Luke asked.

The men nodded and ran up the steps, into the house, where the party was waiting. They closed the door.

"I'm so glad you're home now, Luke!" Baxter came off the porch and hurled himself into Luke's arms. Jasmine started forward, but Luke held up a hand, caught his balance and hugged the boy back.

"Not half as glad as I am, Bax," he said. "But here. I have a little surprise for you. Two, actually. Now, the first one just can't wait, so you'd better take it now. It's in here." He held up the canvas tote bag.

Frowning, Bax parted it on top to look inside. A small brown puppy poked his head out the top and licked Baxter's nose. The boy squealed and scooped it up, hugging it close. "For me? Really, oh, really? Oh, Mom, can I keep him? Can I?"

Jasmine smiled damply, nodding her head hard, meeting Luke's eyes, love brimming from her own. He couldn't quite get used to that. A woman as special as this one, loving him the way she did.

Baxter sat on the steps, holding the squirming pup in his lap.

"I have one more surprise," Luke said. He pulled a document from his pocket, unfolded it. "This."

Baxter got up and handed the puppy to his mom so he could take a look.

"De...cree...of a...a...dop...adop..." He blinked and his eyes widened. "Adoption?" he asked, looking up at Luke.

"Yep. It's a whole lot of big words and legal terms, Bax, but what it means is that from now on, I'm officially your father."

Baxter's little lips quivered. Tears rose up and one fell over. He said, "You...you...you're my dad?" in a high, squeaky voice that wasn't like his own.

Luke nodded. He couldn't really talk just then. He leaned the cane against the porch, lowered himself onto the top step and folded his son into his arms. Baxter was hugging his neck so hard Luke almost couldn't breathe, and his tears were flowing so fast, Luke couldn't hold back his own.

"I've been wishing and wishing you could be my dad, Luke. And it came true. It really came true!" Baxter said.

Jasmine came down the steps, sat down beside Luke and leaned her head on his shoulder.

"From now on, Bax, I'm gonna make all your wishes come true. And your mom's, too. I promise."

He met Jasmine's eyes, saw that they were as wet as his own. She leaned in and kissed him on the lips, and she said, "You've already granted all mine, Luke. Even the ones I never knew I had."

The three of them embraced, and Luke knew he was home. They all were. Home.

* * * * *

Available in August from

JOAN ELLIOTT PICKART

A brand-new, longer-length book
in the bestselling series,

The *Baby Bet*

Party of Three

He was a hard-boiled cop with a child in his care.
She was a woman in need of his protective embrace.
Together they were a family in the making....

Available at your favorite retail outlet.
Only from Silhouette Books

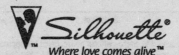

Silhouette®
Where love comes alive™

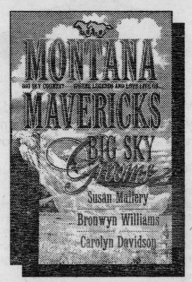
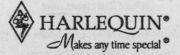